The Stranger Inside

The Stranger Inside

Stories from Beneath the Mirrored Glass

Aziz Saifuddin Mama
Matthew-Donald DeBerardinis Sangster

Published by Mama Sangster Publications in the United States

Some of the material in this book originally appeared, occasionally in different
form, in the blog My New Writings (http://mdsangster.wordpress.com/).

ISBN: 978-0615490540

Printed in the United States of America

10   9   8   7   6   5   4   3   2   1

Cover design by Carolyn Walker - Careiginal Designs ©

Interior illustrations by Jamie Hagerty

Contents

"I believe there is another man
inside every man, a stranger..."

—Wilfred Leland James
(Stephen King's *1922*)

Dedicated to Our Sanity

Our long-lost friend.

The Mirrored Glass

An inward tear greases his spine
his engines roar to a stop.
An instant reversal, a screeching halt.
His time spent, shearing the crop.
His mind encased in glass
A stutter of forbidden mood.
His desire to be one of all,
is forgone as something lewd.
A brittle candle burns soft at night,
it lights the path he'll lonely take.
He sees the beacon of eternal hope
but fears it for he knows it's fake.
He peers upon reflective glass,
to see the love his world holds dear.
Their passion fills his heart with rage
for he fears that it's not sincere.
No love can come from brick-filled eyes
that lay upon forsaken minds.
The ivy for his brazen walls
that he'll hope he finds.
The glass which breaks upon his gaze
shows his heart the pity he knew would come.
He cowers away in infant fear,
he'll block his ears and start to hum.
For this vision he cannot withstand,
because his mind is where it's from.

The Happiness of Roger Stanley

Roger Stanley was a very happy man. He was not deluded by the false allusion of happiness like most other men. Roger had never been accused or convicted of any crime he committed. He was a good Samaritan and always helped out when he could.

Roger was fed three times a day; the meals were always on time, and he never had to ask for them. He was living the high life. Roger Stanley was a very happy man.

Every morning, Roger would wake up to his alarm. He called it his, but "how can you really own anything in this world," he would think. His day was spent sitting in constant reflection until breakfast was served. He would eat his breakfast in silence, occasionally attempting to strike up conversation with his seemingly omnipresent bodyguards. They were the quiet type and were ordered not to talk. He always tried to test them. "Silly guards, one day I'll crack one and then he'll be fired," he would think. His bodyguards took their orders seriously; they barely even talked among each other. Not that Roger would even know; he rarely, if ever, ventured out of his room.

Roger never entertained guests. He was not a fan of people; friendships were always viewed as a distraction. He did, however, have a friend—against his better judgment. Roger could not help taking a liking to Mr. Siber. Roger and Mr. Siber always spoke formally as if they were business partners. It was always "Dr. Stanley" this and "Mr. Siber" that. Roger saw it as a game, a sort of role-playing. Roger did not particularly enjoy engaging in this role-playing; he did not like being called Dr. Stanley. Roger made an exception for Mr. Siber because he deeply enjoyed his company. Mr. Siber rarely withheld anything from Roger because they were so close. Roger believed they both valued the friendship, though Mr. Siber never admitted it.

Aside from occasionally visiting Mr. Siber, Roger spent the time after breakfast humming or thinking of poems. He was quite the creative type, though he rarely got a chance to express it. Even if he were given the opportunity, he wouldn't embrace it. As mentioned before, Roger did not like people. He felt people were not worthy of his words and songs. He did not divulge his creativity to anyone solely because he did not want to. Once lunch was served, he returned to silence. Roger hated noise while he ate. He felt that listening to things while eating detracted from the taste—he liked to focus on one sense at a time.

After lunch, Roger began his meditation. He never had a goal with this meditation, so he was never dissatisfied. He had no need to escape his reality, for his reality was perfect. Roger's meditations were always a form of mindfulness meditation deep-seated in the idea of clairvoyance. It was overwhelmingly peaceful for him. Roger's meditation was always interrupted by the prompt delivery of his dinner which he ate quickly in hopes of regaining his meditative state. His speed was never quick enough.

Occasionally, however, even his dinner was interrupted. Sometimes Mr. Siber called for Roger later in the day. When he did this he always infringed on Roger's dinnertime. Roger always obliged Mr. Siber because he knew it was a rare opportunity he could talk to his friend. Mr. Siber was the warden of a prison and this sincerely fascinated Roger but it also made Mr. Siber's schedule very stringent. During their occasional nighttime meetings, Roger would often ask about the prison. Mr. Siber was never overly enthralled about this topic of conversation but he always allowed it. They had a very open friendship.

Returning to his room, Roger usually sat reflective for several minutes in hopes of retaining his meditative state from before. Accepting the perpetual defeat, Roger would fall asleep to the thoughts that had arisen through his meditation. He would consider this to be an acceptable compromise to the loss of meditative state. Roger followed a strict regiment. He liked it that way. No way for error; no way for unwarranted interruption. He was happy with his life.

Roger Stanley was as free as a man could ever be. He could act in accordance to any desire he wanted by doing whatever he wanted whenever he wanted.

Roger took complete and total advantage of his achieved freedom. He did as he pleased every single day without thought to the repercussions.

Roger continually fed his impulses; anytime a thought entered his mind, he appeased it. His life and the way he lived it epitomized hedonism.

Roger Stanley resided in solitary confinement in Cell Block 3.

Shards of the Mirror

I love to draw. I draw all day long just because it's fun. Sometimes my mommy gets mad at me when I waste my day drawing. But I love to draw. I'm actually drawing a picture of an airplane right now. It's got really pretty wings on it, and I think I'm gonna make it fly to England. The people on it all look so happy except one guy. I don't know why, but he looks real sad for no reason. Planes are so much fun to draw but once I'm done drawing, I never know what to do with the paper; do I finish the drawing and just hang it up? Or do I crumple it up and throw it away?

I'll just put the plane on the ground for now, that sad man is upsetting me.

I feel like drawing a bus now. A big blue city bus driving through New York. There are business people on it and firemen and little old ladies and even a homeless man! He doesn't look like he fits in with his ugly clothes, but they're all people, he belongs on that bus just the same. He looks so much happier than that silly little guy on the plane. But still, I'm bored. There wasn't enough stuff to draw on that bus picture; the homeless man upset me because people don't seem to like him much.

I think I'll just draw a limo. Limos are always fun. Who's ever frowning in a limo? The sun's smiling and the grass is growing and the sky is blue and the limo—the limo is black. I like drawing this limo; the guy in the suit seems really happy; happier than that homeless man on the bus. There are birds chirping and money flying out of the limo. He's so rich! And he seems just so happy! I love the man in the limo, he's even kind of cute; all the ladies must love him.

But now, I have these three drawings and nothing to do with them. I guess I could ask my mommy to hang them up for me but the only one I really like is the Limo. The other two pictures are just sad.

The Stranger Inside

I love to draw. It makes me so happy, but sometimes these stories I make for them get out of hand. The people mess them up, and it upsets me.

Like the man on the plane. I tried to draw him happy but I didn't because the rest of him didn't look happy. He's in a suit but the suit is old, not new like the limo man's suit. He's an older man, and for some reason, he's on this plane to England. I don't know why I think they're going to England, but England seems like a fun place, and the people on the plane look they could use some fun, well at least the sad man does.

The homeless man upsets me because no one likes him. They all look upset because he's stinking up their bus. Mommy tells me "Homeless people are the scum of the earth, they don't belong here and it's our job to remind them." Mommy doesn't like people too much. She throws my drawings out every chance she gets. Well, only when they're pictures of people. I love my drawings. I try to keep as many as I can for as long as I can. But Mommy always finds them eventually.

But I really like the limo man. He's really nice and he seems to be doing well but he's losing lots of money out of his limo. Maybe he's giving it away, I don't know. But he seems real nice, so maybe.

I hope Mommy doesn't find these drawings though. I want some time to make them happy drawings. It makes me sad leaving sad people in my drawings.

* * *

I do not like the smell of this airport.

There is nothing else really with which I could object. The tile floors are clean, the staff is friendly, from the men and women behind the ticket counters to those running security, the place is well lit, there are the appropriate shops and restaurants and food chains, chairs are to be found in plenty by the gates and even around the other parts of the terminal, and there are even a number of somewhat eye-catching, but correctly modest, pieces of modern art on various dais's about the place.

In other words, everything is as it should be. Everything is in its proper aesthetic order. There is not one item, not one aspect of the terminal, not one aspect of the entire airport, not one person that is out of place. All is well-ordered and falling precisely into its proper position.

Everything is aesthetically well-ordered; that is, except for the smell.

It is not a strong smell. It is in fact quite subtle, but I notice it all the same. I am struggling to identify and describe this smell that seems to now follow me about wherever I go, disturbing my previously unperturbed world.

It began . . . well now that I think upon it I'm not exactly sure when it began. About two months ago, if I am not mistaken. I first noticed it in Laura's apartment. At first, I thought that perhaps it had always been present and due to its more subtle odoriferous texture I had simply not noticed it before, but I soon came to suspect that it was a recent addition to Laura's apartment. One which I frowned upon. It ruined the balance, and it ruined the harmony of the entire place. I made mention of this irritating smell to Laura, but she claimed not to smell a thing. As far as she was concerned, there was no smell. I did not agree but decided it was perhaps better to ignore the smell for now (especially seeing as she could not detect a thing and had even become somewhat perturbed with me for suggesting that her apartment could be letting out any sort of unpleasant smell). And so, ignore the smell is precisely what I did.

A good two weeks passed before I noticed the smell again. This time, however, in the vicinity of my closet. I was quite puzzled. That smell had previously only come from Laura's apartment, but now it seemed to be wafting from my own clothing. Clearly, I had come into contact with whatever was causing the smell in Laura's apartment at some point, and in placing my dirty clothes in the hamper within my closet, I had managed to allow the smell to spread.

This too, however, I chose to ignore. Not because I didn't wish to deal with the irritating little smell, which had first caused me to become dissatisfied with Laura's apartment and was now threatening the very closet in which I kept my clothes, but because I assumed that the smell could wait for more important things to be finished first. It was confined to just my closet after all.

A week passed and the smell was never dealt with. Things just kept coming up and preventing me from taking care of it, and I kept putting it off because after all, it was just a little odd scent and was obviously nothing to worry about. That was when I smelled it in the kitchen. Now I had a problem that required immediate attention and was now my top priority.

This smell was now infecting my own apartment, and that was unacceptable. I had been going to Laura's less and less often and started meeting her in public places for dinner nowadays. If a romantic mood struck us both, then we would return to my apartment. We never returned to hers anymore. After having noticed the smell there, I felt the atmosphere of the place ruined, I felt as though something otherwise perfect in its mundane tidiness and order had been marked up and soiled. I no longer took satisfaction in going to Laura's apartment because of that smell. And now that very same smell had followed me home through my clothing and had taken the week to strengthen itself before assaulting other areas of my own apartment. Something had to be done.

I called everyone and anyone under the sun who should have been able to make this slight smell disappear. However, anytime someone arrived to get rid of it, they claimed that they could smell nothing. They shook their heads at me and told me I was imagining things and left the building, feeling as though I had wasted their time.

It was then that I knew that this was a conspiracy, a conspiracy to make me miserable. But who could have been behind it? I did not know.

The Stranger Inside

What I did know was that someone had planted that smell in Laura's apartment for me to eventually notice. And that smell had been brought back to my apartment and was now infecting the entire place. Whereas, I had previously always considered my apartment to be my perfect refuge, my quintessential aesthetic order of how things should be, the one place I could keep in a state of perfection when all else failed, I was now faced with an apartment that was slowly beginning to reek of this subtle yet most distasteful smell. It was agony.

I was becoming depressed. The beauty in the order of the things around me was disappearing. It was all being consumed by this smell. How could I be happy when the simplest of truths were becoming perverted by this pestilential perfume? No matter how much I scrub a table, the smell would just ruin it again. No matter how many times I tried to reorganize my books, the smell made the organization seem chaotic. All the things I had known to be the truths by which I ran my life were now being distorted and altered by the smell. I tried leaving my apartment, but I felt as though the smell would follow me wherever I went. It trailed behind me like a mist of translucent vapor. I knew it was there, I knew it had to be there, I knew *they* had put it there to make me feel this way, but I just couldn't get anyone to believe me.

It was almost two months after I first noticed the smell, and I was sinking further into depression and anxiety. I could not rid myself of this infernal smell, this subtle and almost lovely but just so completely unpleasant smell which was ruining my life. I had to escape *them*, the ones who set it upon me. I don't know who they are, but I know *they* are there, watching me, watching my every move, just waiting for the smell to finally break me down.

I had to escape.

And so here I am. Standing in Terminal C of the international airport, waiting for a plane that will take me to England. The airport still smells, and I do not know if the smell will follow me on to the plane. I can only hope that it cannot do so, because *they* cannot do so. I have been watching the other passengers closely. *They* are not among the passengers. If *they* were here, I would know. The boarding process has begun, time for me to take my seat. The smell of course following is right behind me. I find myself depressed once again. Maybe this plan isn't going to work. Maybe *they* don't have to physically guide the smell anymore. Maybe it can follow me on its own now without them. I don't know what to do, but it is too late to turn back for the plane is lifting off. My fellow passengers, the smell, and I are all bound together now on this plane. I can only pray that *they*, the ones who sent this smell after me, will not be able to find me in England. Perhaps then I can find some solace, some peace, and some happiness once again.

*   *   *

Marshall Whittaker's favorite part of the day was anytime he was asleep. Sleep was all that Marshall ever thought about; he truly cared for practically nothing else. He found reality harsh and distasteful, and so Marshall would take refuge in his dreams, in his sleep. One could say that Marshall was a man who found himself constantly distracted while he was awake. His mind was never truly focused on whatever it was before him, for more often than not Marshall would be thinking of something completely different and completely unrelated to whatever it is that is currently being discussed. In fact, it was Marshall's constant distraction that caused him to finally lose his wife, his two children, his house, and the bank accounts his wife had managed with him. He couldn't really help that he had lost these things. Marshall had other and more important priorities. In the end, he lived almost entirely in his head. Living on the street, having barely any food to eat, wearing raggedy and dirty clothing, none of these things bothered Marshall. As far as he was concerned, he wasn't a homeless and a jobless man, because in his head he was someone else.

The Stranger Inside

One day, it began to rain, but instead of going down into the subway like he normally did, Marshall decided to take a bus. It had been a while since he was on one, and more importantly, he knew the swaying movements of the bus would help put him right to sleep.

A large blue bus, city line number 57, pulled up to the bus stop. One by one, all of the passengers boarded the bus and paid their fare. Marshall quickly found a space for himself in the very back right-hand corner of the bus. This space was easy for him to acquire, considering his appearance and how it would instantly cause most people to be repelled by the sight of him. Marshall spent the first few stops looking at some of the other passengers on the bus that day. The bus was filled with an eclectic collection of different types of people. A few of the passengers were businessmen, clearly making money but not yet able to afford a more luxurious means of transportation. There were some young children on the bus as well, some old enough to ride alone and others with their parents. Two off duty firemen were standing by the bus's one door, talking to each other, and before them a group of old woman dominated the front of the bus.

Marshall soon stopped paying attention to who were on the bus. These people were of little importance to him, and so, he chose to pay them no mind. Marshall was distracted by his inner thoughts. The people on the bus, however, certainly did not stop taking notice of Marshall. Even in this part of the city, Marshall stuck out like a sore thumb. He clearly did not belong to the regular crowd of people who rode the number 57.

Marshall looked like something akin to a great tan and gray blob of torn clothing, unkempt hair, dirty newspaper, and greasy skin poking out here and there. He had also not bathed in some time and so smelled rather badly. While Marshall's appearance caused a great deal of animosity to be directed his way in the form of angry glaring gazes, it was ironically his dirty appearance that prevented his being thrown off the bus as no one wanted to even come near him.

The Stranger Inside

As has already been mentioned, however, Marshall was completely unaware of the hostility being generated due to his presence. He was concerned with an idea, an idea that had crept into his mind when Marshall was just a young man.

If life is so solitary, poor, nasty, *brutish*, and short, why can't a man escape into his dreams? Escape, not just for a night, but forever.

Marshall had at first only thought about this idea in his spare time as a young man in university, studying to become an accountant. It had come to him while reading Dostoevsky's novel *Crime and Punishment*. Marshall had been fascinated with the main character Raskolnikov and his motivation for committing what the character argued was a "righteous" murder. It had seemed to Marshall that Raskolnikov would have been far better off to follow a different dream, hopefully one that wouldn't land Raskolnikov in jail. It was then at that moment when Marshall first thought of the idea in a concrete and explicit sense. Raskolnikov would have been far better to live in his dreams, escape reality in his dreams where he could axe the old pawnbroker over and over again without a single repercussion. Dreams were man's last refuge and best escape as far as Marshall was concerned, so why couldn't a man escape reality forever in his dreams?

It had only seemed like an interesting idea at the time. After all, he was having too much fun in university, learning and enjoying himself. However, in the final year of his undergraduate experience Marshall suffered a rather bad breakup which truly upset him. It was then, during one of Marshall's darkest moments when he could only think about his own emotions of misery that the idea first came to save him. When Marshall was upset and on the verge of complete collapse, the idea rose again in his mind. It was then that Marshall knew that he would never let anything upset him so much again, for if something threatened to do so, he would retreat back into the sanctuary that was his inner mind and let his dreams carry him away to better places.

The Stranger Inside

A few years after university found Marshall employed in a respectable accounting firm and married with a child on the way. He had a nice house, a good wife, and was excited to be a father. Life had been going well for Marshall, so he had not had any need for his idea to come save him from unhappiness. Not yet.

It was November 11. Marshall had been married now for nearly nine years, he had two spoiled and bratty children, a larger house with an even larger mortgage, an unsatisfied wife who he suspected was cheating on him, and he had just been informed that he was going to be laid off as part of the downsizing occurring in the accounting firm he had been working in for over a decade. Marshall was utterly crushed. Work had been his saving grace for most of his married life. When Marshall couldn't stand being at home anymore, he would just go to work. At work, at least he had felt useful, successful, and productive. At work, he had at least made some sort of recognizable contribution. Now, his refuge from the family he was slowly coming to despise was being taken away from him, and things at home were only going to get worse.

It was November 11, and Marshall wanted to kill himself.

He knew how he was going to do it. He would go home, open up the high cupboard in the kitchen where his wife kept her anxiety medication, take the entire bottle of Xanax, and then drive to a motel somewhere nearby. Then he would lie down on the bed and, one by one, take every pill left in the bottle. Marshall thought it was especially ironic, that the medicine that had been supposed to keep his wife in a happier place was about to put him in a happier place far away from her. Marshall thought all of this as he drove home for the last time.

As I'm sure one might have guessed, however, Marshall did not die that night. The great idea came to save him. Marshall was halfway through the bottle of pills when he was suddenly hit by a wave of fatigue, lightheadedness, and a feeling of utter bliss. He had ingested a rather large number of pills by this time after all. It was while in the grip of this feeling that Marshall passed out and started to dream.

Marshall did not wake up for nearly three days.

When he did eventually wake up, Marshall still felt as though he was dreaming. Nothing seemed quite so real to him anymore. Perspectives shifted constantly, nothing that was anything was really itself, and everything was a little hazy. Of two things, however, Marshall was absolutely certain. He was certain that his great idea, so far superior to the poor and foolish great idea of Raskolnikov, was a reason to go on living. He was also certain that those three days spent drifting in the haze of a dream world of his own imagining were the best three days of his life, and he was going to spend the rest of his life trying to find a way back to that dream world.

Marshall did eventually go home. His wife interrogated and screamed at him, but Marshall barely noticed. He was concerned with his inner thoughts, with his great idea. It was only a few short weeks after Marshall had been reborn in that dirty motel when his wife divorced Marshall, took the house, took the car, took the bank accounts, took the children, and left Marshall with nothing.

He barely noticed. He was concerned with his inner thoughts, with his great idea.

The bus hit a bump in the road, and Marshall was jolted awake. He looked about him, not much time had passed for it was roughly the same group of people glaring at him. Marshall leaned his head against the window and looked at the cars and people he could see outside. They were so far removed from him, from what he cared about. Sure they were people like him, but how long had it been since anyone had treated him like a real person since his descent into the depths of poverty? People barely treated Marshall as a human being now. He didn't blame them though for he knew he must appear rather strange. But he didn't really care about other people anymore. In fact, he barely noticed them. He was concerned with his inner thoughts, with his great idea.

* * *

It was 6:00 a.m. on an average day for Paul Friedman. He was like everyone else, in the sense that he was filthy rich for no apparent reason. See, Paul had recently come into some money upon the realization of an accidental investment. When Paul was in college, he had a day of drunken concourse during which he decided to head down to Wall Street to spend his refund check on something smart. So he decided to go about this in the least intelligent way possible, by walking into the New York Stock Exchange and laying some money down on the company with the best name, and by that we mean, the company with a name that could be used as euphemism for sex or sex organs.

Long story short, six months ago Paul Friedman had started receiving dividends from a company he recognized immediately, Google. Apparently, they had been sending the checks to his dorm room, which in his drunken stupor he had signed as his permanent address. Two months ago, the value of the stocks reached such a level that he would never be broke again if he sold then. So doing what any sane man would do, he sold.

Having now this expansive world of lavish riches unfolded to him, he was unsure how to best take advantage of his situation. For this reason, he followed the typical movie ideas for what rich people are supposed to do. He bought a limo.

Paul Friedman was not an unhappy man before coming into money. He was very happy because he had everything he wanted in the world. For this reason, when he came into money, he had no desire to spend it. All of his fiscal urges were fulfilled, and he had no real unsubstantiated worries in the world. He was in a place of happiness. The money was just gravy on the mashed potatoes that were his life.

The Stranger Inside

Paul Friedman had just entered his brand new state-of-the-art limousine when he received the phone call. His mother had just passed away. She had fought a long tragic war with breast cancer, but even the Friedman's newly acquired wealth was no match for it. After hearing of this news he entered his limousine regardless. The driver, Fernando, noticed the sudden change in Paul's demeanor and rightfully questioned him,

"I see you just got off the phone and now you're upset. Bad news, sir?"

"My mother has passed."

"I know this is out of my general code of service, but would you like to talk about it?"

"Not really, Fernando. Not because it's overly distressing, but because it's not."

"Were you and your mother not close?"

"No, we were, as you say, thick as thieves. Death, however, is an inevitability and must be seen as such. Nothing is permanent, and we must celebrate. I've known for years she was going to die sooner or later, though I was hoping for later, I knew it would be sooner."

"I guess I understand, sir. Shall I take you to your work?"

"Well, though I may not seem distressed by this news, we *will* be altering the day's course of activities. Take me down to Times Square. I want to see the morning commute for what it really is. As you can tell, there is no rush."

"Right on it, sir. Or well, *not* right on it."

Fernando drove Paul Friedman down to Times Square to watch the previously fabled New York morning commute. Paul had never had to experience this because he was a graphic designer. He worked out of his own apartment and worked his own hours, even before the money came. It goes without saying, the money helped, it really did.

The Stranger Inside

On this trek, Paul got to thinking about life and death. The meaning between the two and why people always separate them, "they are so similar, they are practically the same idea," he thought.

And so he questions his faithful driver,

"Fernando, have you ever thought about your life?"

"Why yes, sir, it's all I ever do. I think about how my job supports my family and that's why I do it, I think about how I wish I could afford fancy food for my family, I think about how I even wish to be able to afford the very suit I'm wearing."

"No, I believe you've mistaken me. Those are thoughts about money. Not about life, your life, your meaning."

"Well, I never thought I was meant to be a limo driver if that's what you're asking."

"I guess I don't really know what I'm asking, Fernando, I'm sorry I bothered you."

"Never apologize to me, sir; you're putting my son through college."

Paul Friedman really didn't know what he was asking but he knew he was breaking ground. He knew something inside of him was changing. He knew something deep inside was opening up. He knew that it had to do with that unanswerable question.

This journey took longer than either Paul or Fernando had anticipated. Fernando feared they would soon run out of gas; Paul feared nothing. Paul was not an ordinary child, he had no fear of the dark or heights or even clowns. He did not fear these things because they were tangible, they were testable. He would think,

"The dark cannot harm me, only things in the dark can harm me, and if they try, I will deal with it as they rush me. Heights are only frightening if you fall from them, it's only the impact upon the fall that I fear, and if I encounter that I can deal with it then. Spiders do not harm me unless provoked, and most spiders are harmless regardless. But if I decide one day to provoke a 'dreaded spider,' I will deal with the spider then, the best way I know how, by crushing it."

The only thing Paul ever feared was mirrors. He could never really understand why, until one day, he had found a shattered mirror on the ground. It was a fancy mirror, sparkling glass inlayed into sterling silver.

"Only rich people have ever held this mirror," he would think to himself.

He looked at his reflection in this shattered mirror, which he rarely did. He noticed something different about his face; he did not recognize it anymore. He threw the mirror and ran.

It was never the mirror that frightened Paul. It was the change that it could present. It was never the mirror itself as he so illogically thought. It was this idea that change could happen without warning and that a tool is required to even notice it.

The fear had finally left Fernando when they rolled upon seemingly the only gas station in all of New York. While Fernando was pumping the gas Paul had another thought,

"Why is life so morbid?"

Fernando hastily replies, "Sir, I don't know. Because death is, I suppose."

"But then, why is the life that precedes it so depressing and grim? I see all these people with their sorrows and their misery but none of it amounts to anything. Death is inevitable, sure, but life is only death if not lived."

"Sir, I guess you are right. But what is with this change of mind, are you sure your mother's passing has not upset you?"

"No, sir, not at all. If anything, it has enlightened me, I have felt this way for years but always assumed that others felt this way too. I guess I must be the only one that sees death in this way."

Fernando finished pumping the gas and reentered Paul's anything-but-humble limo.

"Sir, would you still like me to head downtown?"

Fernando questions whether or not Paul really wants to see the commute.

"How else will I find out if I'm the only one like me?"

Paul Friedman finally reached his destination. Times Square was finally in sight. He bellowed to Fernando to get in the slowest lane. Fernando obliged. Paul then exited the moving limo to retrieve two giant trash bags that were in the trunk. Fernando looked on questioningly as Paul reentered the limo.

"Mr. Friedman, if you don't mind me asking, since when were those bags in the trunk?"

"I knew this day was coming, Fernando, I had to prepare."

Upon these words, Paul Friedman opened his sunroof and released his fortune unto the world.

*　　*　　*

The nurse, clad in her asylum issue scrubs, makes her daily round. As she passes room 42, she hears a fit of joy occurring and feels the necessity to check in on the most recent addition to the ward. Upon entering, she becomes enraged with the patient.

"Joshua, how many times must I tell you? You are not fit to draw again. You do not understand the ramifications of your actions. Your drawings are always so morbid, and you make these people out to have such pathetic existences. You are not of right mind to play games with people's lives."

"But, Mommy, I love to draw, it makes me happy. Look how happy the people on the bus are!"

"Yes but, Joshua, look at him and his despair, once you learn your lesson you can draw again, but until then I'm going to have to take these away."

"But, Mommy!"

"No 'buts,' Joshua."

The Stranger Inside

The nurse gathers his drawings and crumples them up. She closes the door to his room and tosses the drawings in the nearest bin.

* * *

What is happening to me? I am so lost, I . . .

. . . am on the . . .

. . . was on the plane? The smell was following me and I was . . .

. . . running? Flashes of color, it's too bright. Can't see, can't feel, the plane is . . .

. . . folding? On itself and in itself melting into and out of . . .

. . . my skin? But how?

Pain. I feel pain. Horror. Agony. My arm is breaking and melting and folding, and I scream but there is no sound. I have no mouth. No eyes. I am . . . not. Horrendous agony. Why? Passengers are gone. Destroyed, melted, crumpled, broken, gone. Have *they* gone too? Screams. Lightning bolt pain streaking, in and around what was/is/won't be? . . . me.

I am . . .

. . . gone? Oblivion.

The smell is . . .

. . . gone? Ecstasy.

* * *

Marshall suddenly began to convulse. Shaking violently, he all of a sudden experienced true physical agony for the first time in his life. He is dying. He knows this but doesn't know this. The bus seems to contort around him, using him as the focal point of some strange and hideous vortex, twisting and breaking the bus and its passengers into some grand amalgamation of flesh, blood, bone, metal, color, fear, heat, pain,

25

screams, and ripped clothing. Marshall is no longer Marshall. He barely is anything. He doesn't have long. Soon Marshall, the passengers who so loathed him, the bus, the driver, and Marshall's entire world will be gone. Ripped, torn, crumpled, destroyed, and tossed aside like so much useless garbage. Marshall is almost gone now. He doesn't scream or struggle anymore. He believes he is traveling, traveling into his great idea. He sees darkness creep into what is left of his vision and believes it is merely the beginning of a most perfect end. He thinks that soon, he will be able to dream forever.

Marshall's last thought right before the end was one simple word: "Finally."

* * *

I'm sad Mommy always takes my drawings. I love them, doesn't she see this? But she doesn't know I got to keep one drawing, Mr. Limo-Man as I have started to call him. I love Mr. Limo-Man. He's always so happy. I will keep his drawing under my pillow; maybe she won't find it there.

No Solace for Restless Men

"Shit. I'm going to be late for this meeting."

Rattling noises of the subway train mingle with the quiet chatter of the regular commuters as Mr. Mordent curses silently to himself.

"I've never been late. Not once."

He looks at his watch for the umpteenth time, its face reflecting the subtle shifts in light thrown into the train by the rapidly flashing advertisements on the wall of the subway tunnel.

"Shit. This is so embarrassing."

Creaky squeals of the wheels along the tracks signal the slowing of the train at the stop where Mr. Mordent must disembark. The train lurches to a halt, and for a moment, time freezes as the expectant passengers wait for the doors. Then, with a quick intake of air and a whirring sound, the doors open, allowing the huddled masses aboard the train to bolt out and dash toward wherever it is they think they have to be.

Mr. Mordent rushes into the financial district to his company's building. He hops into the elevator and presses the button for the eleventh floor repeatedly, as though this would somehow make the elevator move faster.

"Come on shut the doors already, damn it. Don't make me any later then I am."

Mr. Mordent looks around the elevator at the other people clustered inside. No one he knows, no one he would be forced to exchange a perfunctory hello with. No one is speaking, the silence broken only by the droning of the vapid jazz that the elevator pumps out of its speakers.

The Stranger Inside

Mr. Mordent is thankful for the background noise. It keeps him from having to think.

A beep and the electronic voice of a bored woman herald the arrival of the eleventh floor. The elevator doors open, and Mr. Mordent rushes to his office to pick up the briefing papers he is supposed to be presenting at the meeting.

"What in the hell is this?"

Mr. Mordent stands in puzzlement. His office door is wide open, the office is empty, his desk is cleared, and all of his things are gone. Nothing remains in the room except a neglected lamp sitting unplugged in the corner, his name tag on his desk, and a few empty cardboard boxes to the right of the door.

"What's happened to my office? I can't have been fired; that's simply impossible. Maybe there was a leak or something, and they had to move me? Fuck if I know, doesn't matter, no time. I need those briefing papers. Mark must have them."

Mr. Mordent rushes away from the mystery that is his empty office and heads toward his colleague's office down the hall. Mr. Mordent is in such a rush that he doesn't notice the strange looks he receives from several of the people in the office as he passes by.

Mr. Mordent arrives at his colleague's office only to find that Mark is not there.

"Hey is Mark in? I need some briefing papers from him for the meeting."

"No, sir, I'm afraid he isn't in at the moment. Would you like me to leave Mr. Calridge a message? Or perhaps you would like to wait for him? He should be returning fairly soon."

"No. I can't, no time. He must already be in the meeting. I'll meet him there."

The Stranger Inside

Mr. Mordent rushes off once again, only now in the direction of Meeting Room C where he and Mark are supposed to be giving a presentation. When halfway to the meeting room Mr. Mordent suddenly finds himself puzzled.

"That was odd. Irene was pretty formal back there. Treated me like I was just some other client. Oh well, no time for that now I have to get to the meeting. She's probably just having a bad day."

After several twists and turns in the office hallways, Mr. Mordent now finds himself staring down the corridor at the door to the meeting room. He takes a moment to slow his pace and adjust his tie and run his hand through his hair. Then, with quick rapid strides, he comes face to face with the door and throws it open.

"So sorry I'm late everyone it was a nightmare trying to . . ."

Mr. Mordent stops midway through his prepared apology and defamation of the New York public transportation system and is struck now with mounting confusion. The meeting room is completely empty. Mark is not there. The members of the board are not there. No one is there. For a few cold seconds, Mr. Mordent is frozen in place and struck with creeping self-doubt.

"It was set for Meeting Room C at eight thirty. What on earth is going on?"

Mr. Mordent looks about the room once again, unable to understand the emptiness before him.

"This makes no sense, they couldn't have finished already; the presentation was going to take at least two hours. Maybe it got moved to a different room. That's it! They must have switched rooms."

With this thought, Mr. Mordent dashes out of Meeting Room C and frantically checks all of the other meeting rooms down the corridor. He finds nothing and no one in any of them. His confusion is even greater now. For a few precious minutes, he stands in the middle of the hallway, his right hand holding the side of his head, and looks about in bewilderment.

"I need to talk to the boss. Why has the meeting been cancelled? And why is my office empty? Shit, these are too many questions. I'll talk to the boss, he will know what's going on."

With this numbing thought employed to steady his mind, Mr. Mordent rushes back to the elevators so he can get to the twelfth floor.

"That's odd, there's no elevator music playing. I don't like that, this is far too quiet."

Mr. Mordent finds himself fidgeting awkwardly in an attempt to take his mind of off the silence pervading in the elevator. Thankfully, the trip up one floor was brief. As the elevator doors opened and Mr. Mordent rushed out toward his boss's office, an acquaintance passed by him and headed into the elevator.

"Hey, Steve, how are you?"

The acquaintance turns sharply to look back at who greeted him and stares at the receding figure of Mr. Mordent as he rushes away.

"Who the hell was that guy?"

Pushing open the large and opaque door that lead to the boss's waiting room, Mr. Mordent was struck by the figure of a woman he did not recognize sitting at the reception desk.

"That's strange, I wonder where Anne is? She's not supposed to be retiring for another four days. No matter, I just need to see the boss."

The receptionist who was not Anne swiveled in her chair and turned toward Mr. Mordent as he approached the desk.

"Hello, sir, how can I help you?"

"Is the boss in?"

"No, sir, I'm afraid he is out with a client at the moment and will not be returning until much later in the day. Would you like me to take a message for you to leave with Mr. Novorov?"

"No, no, I will speak to him myself later."

"Very well, sir, you have a pleasant day."

Mr. Mordent turned on his heels and walked out of the waiting room, his right hand holding the side of his head.

"Okay. So I was late to work, my office has been cleared, Mark wasn't in his office, the meeting wasn't where it was supposed to be, and now the boss is unavailable for the rest of the day? What in God's name is going on?"

Habit had brought Mr. Mordent back to the elevators. Realizing he was standing in front of them, he pressed the down button. Mr. Mordent was so lost in thought that the elevator doors stood open before him for so long that they began to shut again. Finally taking notice of the elevator doors, Mr. Mordent squeezed himself into the elevator and pressed the button for the eleventh floor. While in the elevator, Mr. Mordent's confusion and doubt was quickly escalating to fear and panic.

"Something is happening. Something is going on that I don't know about. What is it? I should have been informed if the meeting was cancelled or rescheduled. The boss wasn't supposed to be out seeing clients today; he was supposed to be here. Why did Irene treat me like I don't belong? Why the hell is my office empty? Something's going on. I need to find out what."

The elevator doors open, Mr. Mordent takes a few hesitant steps and then pauses.

"I have to find Mark. I need to know what is going on."

With renewed vigor, Mr. Mordent practically runs down the hallway toward Mark's office. Despite his rush, Mr. Mordent's urgent and fear-ridden sense of panic causes him to finally take notice of the strange looks he receives from several of the people in the office as he passes by. Placing his right hand on the side of his head, he quickens his already frenetic pace.

The Stranger Inside

"They are all staring at me. Something is going on. And they all know what it is."

His mouth twisted into a grimace of fear, Mr. Mordent reaches Mark's office and marches up to Irene.

"I need to see Mark right away."

"I'm sorry, sir, but he just went in the office with a client I'm afraid you will have to wait. Please feel free to take a seat just there."

"Irene! This is really important! I need to see Mark now!"

"Sir, I ask you to lower your voice and not be so bold as to call me by my first name."

"Bold! Irene what in God's name are you talking about being so bold?"

"Sir, I am asking you for the last time to lower you voice."

"Good god, woman, what is wrong with you? What is wrong with everyone today? You're acting like you don't even know me!"

"Sir, I don't know you. I have never seen you before in my life. Please calm yourself and lower your voice."

Mr. Mordent has been struck dumb. Beads of sweat have begun to trickle down the side of his face, and he becomes very pale. He once again places his right hand on the side of his face and staggers backward several feet.

"Sir? Are you well?"

"This can't be happening. This can't be happening to me."

"Sir, is everything all right?"

"No, Irene! Nothing is all right! How can you say you don't know who I am? I've known you since you came to work for Mark last year! It's me, Jim! Jim Mordent!"

A dark cloud of anger suddenly passes over Irene's face. Her cheeks become flushed and tears begin to well up in the corner of her eyes. She slowly raises herself up out of her seat and glares at Mr. Mordent intensely. This is not a response that he was anticipating, and he is shocked and taken aback.

"Irene . . ."

"Don't you dare call me by my first name! I don't know who you are or what game you're playing at but what you are doing is not funny. It's sick! It's revolting! Jim Mordent was a good friend of mine and a friend of Mr. Calridge and your behavior, sir, is an utter disgrace to his memory."

"A disgrace to his memory?"

"Yes a disgrace! An utter disgrace. Jim Mordent was struck by a car when crossing the street and died four days ago. You are not him!"

"Hit by a car?"

"Sir, I am asking you one time and one time only to leave this building immediately. If you don't then I will call security."

Mr. Mordent's world has just been shattered. He runs like a man possessed out of the building and out into the street. Once in the street, he keeps running. He does not head in any particular direction, he simply flails about. He has been reduced to a state of utter hysteria and is firmly in the grip of a cold and agonizing terror. Holding the side of his face with his right hand, he stumbles about, his mind in a state of absolute chaos.

"Dead? No I am not dead. I'm not. I can't be. There was no car, I didn't get hit by a car, I'm not dead. I can't be! I'm right here, walking around. They can see me, they are all staring at me. I'm not dead. I can't be! . . . Can I?"

Mr. Mordent suddenly found himself staring into an entrance to the subway. Without thinking, he walks down and gets on the first subway train that he sees. He goes to the corner and sits down. Slowly, he is able to calm himself. His thoughts, though still panicked, are slowly becoming more ordered.

The Stranger Inside

"Okay. I need to think this through. This is something that I can figure out. I'm not dead. I'm right here. There has to be a reason for this. I can figure this out."

Mr. Mordent is finally able to achieve a state of calm. He is a man used to constant movement, constant busyness. Now, he turns his penchant for constant physical movement inward and applies it to his mind for the first time.

"I will figure this out. I am going to sit right here in this spot and remember everything that has happened to me in the last four days. There is no way that I'm dead, no matter what anyone says. I can prove that to myself. And I'll sit here until I do."

Still holding the side of his face with his right hand, Mr. Mordent began to think.

* * *

"God damn it, George, hurry up. If we miss this one, we're going to be late."

"I'm coming, I'm coming!"

"Shit that was close, the door shut just behind you."

"Yeah well, we made it didn't we?"

"We'll have made it when we actually get to the meeting on time."

"Hey look at that."

"Look at what?"

"That guy who's always in the corner, the Thinker, he's gone."

"What guy?"

"You know, every time we get on the train there's always that one guy sitting in the corner holding his head and staring out into space. Looks like that Rodin sculpture you know?"

"Yeah, so what?"

"Well he's gone. I mean, he's been sitting there every day since we started at the firm. He was almost part of the landscape of the train. Now he's gone. I wonder where he is."

"Who gives a fuck?"

Freedom
Bereaved

And they come to Jesus, and

see

him that was possessed with the devil,
and had the legion, sitting, and clothed,
and in his right mind;

and they were afraid.

—Mark 5:15

*   *   *

"This is the best part of my entire day," Thomas thought to himself as he looked around the bar, "I feel more relaxed here than I ever could at home."

The bar, the Albatross, was located off the main road of the town. You wouldn't notice the entrance were it not for the flickering neon sign hanging above the door. The inside wasn't overly large, but had enough room to accommodate the many regulars who, like Thomas, came to the bar seeking refuge.

Thomas shifted around on his seat, trying to make himself a little more comfortable. He looked around at the familiar scene of the bar, and eventually his eyes came to rest on his now empty glass. Thomas waved at the barkeep, "Hey, another scotch on the rocks."

"Starting your seventh I see," spoke a man Thomas had never seen before.

"What?"

"This has become a regular occurrence for you, hasn't it?"

"Yeah it has, wait what . . . do I know you?"

The Stranger Inside

"You don't know me, but I know you better than you know yourself."

Thomas sat reflective while sipping on his scotch. The seasoned middle-aged man had taken residence upon the tattered stool beside Thomas with his martini in hand. Thomas finally broke out of his extended pensive state.

"How could you possibly know me? I've been thinking, and I'm sure that I've never seen you before in my life."

"And that is what I've said. You don't know me, but I know your type, son. You're a family man by definition, and you immerse yourself into that with every thought and action," the man said, smiling slightly, "Would you like to talk about them?"

"No, they're the last thing on my mind."

He then questioned Thomas, with an expression on his face that almost made it seem as though he already knew the answer, "Oh really, well then what is currently occupying your thoughts?"

"I don't know. Things I'm afraid of I guess . . . I don't know where I'm going with my life. I don't know why I even get up in the morning anymore," said Thomas, still in shock over the situation and speaking more to himself than to anyone else.

"I can see this, but why do you think these thoughts are plaguing you?"

"I don't know man . . . but I just want them to go away." Thomas said as he finished his drink. Gesturing to his empty glass, "But I guess that's my cue to go home."

"If that's your choice, so be it, but you'll be back soon."

"What do you mean?"

"I expect that what issues you may be experiencing will escalate to new levels, and when they do, I'll be seeing you again." The man stood from his stool and began to walk toward the exit.

"Wait, who are you? I don't even know your name!" Thomas bellowed after the man.

The Stranger Inside

Not hearing Thomas's question, the man instantly regretted his decision to leave behind his glass. He turned back to grab his martini from the bar and noticed that Thomas was awaiting some sort of response.

Anticipating the inevitable question on Thomas's mind, he replied, "My name is Walter."

Walter then sauntered out the door and disappeared into the night.

Thomas, recounting his replete yet transient conversation, found himself relaxing for once. Grinning to himself he sat in reflection, "And I thought I was confused before."

*   *   *

The next night, Thomas reenters the bar with one goal on his mind: freedom from his thoughts. To do so, he went about it the only way he could think of: complete and utter inebriation. Thomas went to the bar several hours before the neon sign would normally call to him, due to this all-encompassing goal. Some time and many glasses later, Thomas rejoined the familiar ground of his favorite stool. He was interrupted from his perpetual self-loathing when the seemingly ever-present Walter approached him.

"I knew I would see you again."

Startled by the abrupt ending to his contemplation, Thomas accidentally divulged his thoughts, "How could they possible leave *me*. Oh, Walter, I didn't see you there."

"So I take it your family finally had enough of your shenanigans."

"I don't even know. I came back last night, and they were gone. No note, no explanation, nothing. How could they do this so close to Christmas? I love them for everything they give me but . . . I don't know . . . it's just hard sometimes, and I guess it started to show. Wait, you knew this was going to happen? How?"

"I told you before that I know your kind, Thomas, but I'm sure anyone in this bar could've seen this coming."

"I guess it *is* kind of written on my face," said Thomas, holding his head in his hands, "Walter, they gave me meaning. My family is who I am and they always have been. I don't know what I'm going to do now."

"If they were so important, then why did you feel it necessary to escape them? After all, you frequent this bar with a greater regularity than almost anyone else."

Thomas, adding another empty glass to his voluminous collection, expelled, "They just held me back, man. I was constricted by them . . . I could never do what I wanted to do."

Walter, as if shepherding Thomas toward something he had not yet grasped, rousingly questioned, "Well, what *do* you want?"

"I don't know! I guess I just want to be free for once."

"Is that what you really want, do you really want that responsibility?"

"I don't know what you mean by responsibility, I want to be free of everything. I want to just get away from the pressure my family put on me, and I guess now I have that chance since they're gone."

"You don't sound too enthralled with this opportunity."

"Well, you've got me second-guessing with that mention of responsibility. How can I have responsibility if I'm free? Isn't someone who's free . . . well . . . free of constraints?"

"Actualized freedom is inherently coupled with responsibility. Only through ultimate freedom can you escape that burden. But ultimate freedom is just that, an ultimatum; it is a sincere and utter devotion to the cause of releasing yourself and becoming free."

"I still don't understand at all, how can you be free and responsible at the same time?"

"A man sits alone with no one questioning him; he is left to be with his thoughts. He is free to act as he pleases. He is fed ritually every morning, noon, and night by someone whose job it is to do so. He is free to see whomever he likes, whenever he likes, and do whatever he so chooses to do with them. Is this man not free?"

"Well yeah, if he can do whatever he wants, he is free."

"What if I were to tell you that this man resides in prison, more specifically in solitary confinement?"

"That can't be possible. You said he was free to do as he wishes. Prisoners aren't free to do anything."

"It is the devotion to the idea that makes its practice possible. I see now that you are not yet devoted to the idea of freedom, but it will come in time, Thomas. So that being the case, what is it that you truly want?"

"You think low of me, Walter. But I guess all I know is that whatever I might have really wanted was crushed by my family's stifling demands."

"I don't think low of you, Thomas; I wouldn't talk to you if I did. You will, however, soon realize that no one can understand you. People will try, but no one will really grasp your essence. The cares of a family man are allusive indeed."

"Don't you mean illusive?"

"I choose my words carefully, son. Though you say you want something more, you'll never know what else there is until you shed your old perceptions."

"I guess I understand . . . But I still don't know how you could 'know me better than I know myself.'"

Walter, still nursing his seemingly endless glass, asserted, "The future is not something to perceive or to hope for; it is an inevitability to either accept or to change. Your future is laid out, but just knowing that presents the opportunity to alter it."

"You didn't answer my question."

"You didn't ask one."

Walter stood up from the bar, remembering to take his glass, and strode out of sight.

The Stranger Inside

Thomas, again perplexed at the preceding conversation, uttered to himself, "Even if I was sober, I'd still call bullshit."

* * *

Several nights later, Thomas found himself slaving over his usual scotch on the rocks on his usual stool. He had built a ritual that consumed his day ever since the disappearance of his family. Wake up at two. Eat. Watch TV. Nap. Look at old photo albums. Eat. Walk to the bar. Go home. Sleep. Repeat. This day, however, did not quite follow this routine. Thomas woke up early and went for a run around the block. He went to the library to check out a book and ended up reading it in its entirety. He spent his afternoon away from his house for the first time in days. This Christmas Day would forever be burned in Thomas's mind.

Each time Thomas entered the bar, he never spoke to anyone. Walter did not cross Thomas's mind either; he had not taken too kindly to Walter's remarks during their last conversation. As it were, Walter was nowhere to be found anyway. That is, until this particular night. Walter, with strict diligence, approached Thomas and reprimanded him, "I thought you wanted freedom. You have that opportunity now, and yet you do nothing. I thought you wanted to change."

Thomas, startled by the accusation, hastily replied, "I have changed . . . Well, at least I started to, sort of . . . today."

"You think that is change? And yet you are here, of all places, on Christmas night drinking your poignant yet ostentatious single-malt Scotch whisky. You still use your whisky as a moat, to block out all your pain. How can you say that you've changed when everything about you still defines you as you were before your family left?"

"It's just hard, okay? It's hard to be in that empty house all day and have all these old memories glaring me in the face. It's Christmas for Christ's sake. Do you have a family, Walter?"

"To ask a question you don't already know, or at the very least cannot anticipate, the answer of is to take a blind leap of faith in the person you are questioning. Can you really afford any more blind leaps?"

"When you put it that way, I guess not. But I'm still stuck on your opinions about freedom. I've thought about what you said so much, and I still haven't gotten anywhere."

Walter ordered a martini from the barkeep, in an attempt to allot time to garner his thoughts. He calmly replied, "Firstly, they are not merely opinions. To quote a man of more perspicacity than I, 'Reality is the original Rorschach.' Since nothing can truly be fact, isn't everything fact? But I digress. There is no way for me to spell out real freedom to you. I cannot explain what I have not yet fully experienced."

"Then how can anything you say about it be relied on?" Thomas angrily protested.

Receiving his martini, Walter tasted it. Smiling to himself in satisfaction, he placed it on the bar. Walter, almost forgetting a question had been posed to him, replied, "I am not here to achieve it for myself Thomas. The closest I will ever come is when I see it burned in the eyes of someone who has just realized the meaning of ultimate freedom. In the end, what determines a preacher's strength is not the words he says but the people those words affect."

"I guess I see what you're saying. Along the lines of 'those who can't do, teach,' right?" Thomas said sarcastically.

"In all essence, yes. But I must make tonight's meeting brief, for I have an impact to make elsewhere."

"Oh okay, I guess I'll see you?"

"Yes you will, and soon. However, it will be by no accident; once the realization of your deluded debacle occurs, I will be there to join in the celebration. Merry Christmas, Thomas." Walter departed as promptly as he had arrived, but without a thought this time to the glass on the bar.

The Stranger Inside

Thomas, continually riddled by Walter's strange mannerisms, pondered aloud to the forgiving night, "How can a debacle be something to celebrate?"

*   *   *

Once Thomas was forced out of his house after the accident, he moved into a slightly run-down apartment. The police told him that a drunk driver had veered off the road and ended up crashing through Thomas's house eventually coming to rest where Thomas's bed once was. Apparently, this sort of thing was of regular occurrence on Christmas night. It was also mentioned that if the bed had not been there to cushion the impact, the driver would not have survived. Thomas did not view the event with such optimism, however. After all, the driver had disappeared without a trace, and his house was now uninhabitable.

Once it was established that his house would not be suitable to live in for some time, he found the apartment downtown. Thomas soon found himself rekindling old memories by frequenting the largest staple of his past, the Albatross. However, Thomas began to order new drinks and began consistently imbibing more than ever before. He continued trying to find "the new Thomas" at the bottom of a glass, but to no avail. When a drink failed him, he moved on to the next one in hopes that this one would complement the way he had now begun to view himself. Thomas was changed, or at least he thought so. He refused to let anything define him. It was as though starting anew in his raggedy apartment had allowed Thomas the ability to finally change himself. He was his own man.

Thomas had picked a new seat in the bar to claim as his own instead of returning to the barstool he had occupied in the past. This seat had a better view of the bar in general and, as a result, more people could see him now. Thomas had also begun to amass a small group of peers he could willingly refer to as friends, a term he'd never really been able to use before. On this particular evening, these friends were planning a surprise housewarming and New Year's Eve party for their friend as he sat alone in the once-desolate bar of his past. Instead of keeping to himself as he once did, he spoke to the people around him and even struck up conversations with the barkeep, who, he found out, actually lived a street away from his old house. Tom, as his friends would refer to him, was now a fun-loving man. He was given a chance to reinvent himself, and he embraced it. He was slowly becoming hedonism personified.

Walter had not been seen or heard from since his precocious departure the last time the two had met. Tom had begun to think that he had learned whatever lesson Walter was trying to teach and that he probably wouldn't encounter Walter again. Tom had always had a history of being gravely mistaken.

Perched upon his newly claimed seat, Tom ordered the next drink on his agenda—a gin and tonic. Tom was taken aback when the hand that delivered his drink was not the young manicured hand of the barkeep he had expected, but the wrinkled hand of a man he could easily recognize.

"Walter! Long time no see, man, how have you been?"

"Well enough, Thomas, but I think the real question is how have you been?"

"Please, Walter, call me Tom, all my friends do."

All expression on Walter's face was almost immediately quelled. This brief change in Walter's expression went unnoticed by Tom. Walter then began to drink his martini. Tom added, "I've been surprisingly good lately. I've been drinking out of celebration instead of desperation. I never would have thought that all it would take to change my ways would be moving out of my old house. I have friends now, and people in my life that don't restrict me. I can really do whatever I want whenever I want! And it's all thanks to you, you've helped me so much Walter."

Walter faintly remarked, "More so than you know, Tom."

Tom continued, "I was actually wondering if I would ever see you again; you only seem to appear when I'm having issues or I'm distressed."

Walter, not paying attention to Tom's gratitude, questioned him, "Tom, do you believe you've changed? Do you believe you're truly free now?"

"Well, yeah, of course I've changed. Don't you think so?"

"No, I don't believe so in the least. You are different, that is sure. But no, you have not changed at all."

"How can you say that? I have friends now and I'm not restricted anymore. I'm finally free. Or . . . what did you say . . . I've reached 'ultimate freedom.'"

"No , Tom, you are not even free. You still haven't the faintest idea of freedom. Why did you come here today?"

"Just to reminisce, I was . . . I don't know . . . I guess I just missed my family a bit, and this place always comforted me."

"And there it is. Your personal prison. The reason you'll never be truly free."

"But I thought you said the man in the prison was free?" Tom replied, glaring into the bottom of his now empty glass. Tom called for the barkeep and ordered a Jack and Ginger.

"I said nothing. You, however, said a man in prison cannot be free."

"But Walter, I am free. I'm completely changed; I'm a new man entirely."

"You are nothing of the sort. What is the difference between red and green apples? Though they taste different and look different, are they not both apples? Difference is not change."

"You don't have a clue what you're talking about." Tom's temper was rising. With his now-empty glass in hand, Tom exited the bar.

"I am changed!" Tom screamed into the once-forgiving night, throwing his glass at the neon sign.

The Stranger Inside

Tom did not let Walter's remarks affect him. He was changed and he knew it. On the day of New Year's Eve, Tom was nowhere to be found. He spent the day walking around his old neighborhood hoping to find some proof that Walter was wrong—just in case he ever encountered him again. Walter's remarks did not affect him.

Tom found himself retracing the steps he would once take from the bar. He would stumble past his mailbox covered in finger-painted depictions of the members of his family. His path continued past the shed which was full of tools Tom barely knew how to use. This led him around the house he always knew would be too small for a family and then to the back door so as to not wake his wife when he staggered in late at night. He would finally come to rest on the pullout couch in the living room and bring an end to whatever commotion he may have caused.

It was there that Tom slept, on this day, for several hours. Tom had not slept well in his new apartment, it was uptown, and the sounds of the city kept him up. Here in the suburbs, he could sleep; it was peaceful here. Tom awoke to the sounds of cars honking. It was getting dark out, and there were children in the street throwing snowballs and obstructing traffic. "Now that's true freedom. Not a care in the world. It doesn't matter to them that they can't drive yet. Those kids aren't even fazed by the scene they're creating," Tom said to himself.

"Now you understand, Tom."

Not expecting a reply, Tom jumped off the couch, arming himself with the photo album he had fallen asleep with.

"Who's there?" he screamed into the empty caverns of his house.

"It's just me," Walter said, walking through Tom's bedroom door, placing his leather bag on the ground.

"Why are you here? How did you know where my house was?"

"It's less of a matter of why I am here and more of why you are."

The Stranger Inside

"I guess it was a sort of drunken autopilot. My mind kinda just took me here. I haven't really been sleeping well in my apartment anyway."

"Obviously not, Tom, it's the city, and you are not a city man. You are a family man, it's why you are clutching a photo album and not defending yourself with the fire poker that was but a foot further."

Looking back to assess Walter's claim, he said, "I'm done arguing about this, I'm done defending myself. But you still haven't answered me. How did you know where this place was? How did you know this was my house?"

"Some things are better left unknown," Walter said, hoping to drop the subject.

"Walter! Tell me now!" Tom snapped. He had lost his patience with Walter and his ambiguous responses.

"Calm down, Tom, I will tell you. The night we met, I knew you. I knew what you were going through, and I knew the only way you could ever be free. I knew that you could never be free while your family still controlled you."

Tom impatiently interjected, "What are you getting at, Walter, out with it already!"

Walter sat down. "I did what had to be done, Tom."

Tom, bordering fury, interrogated, "Enough of this vague bullshit! What are you talking about?"

Walter, knowing the inevitable, told Tom, "The only path to freedom is paired with difficult decisions. I simply took care of one of those decisions for you."

"You're the reason they left me? What did you say to them?"

"I did not say anything to them."

"If you are the reason they left, but you said nothing to them, why did they disappear? How could they have . . ." Tom couldn't finish his sentence. He had suddenly lost his ability to speak.

Walter placidly replied, "I am the reason that they will not bother you again. I gave you the means to be eternally free of them."

49

Tom could not command his voice or his whole body for that matter. The realization of what Walter had done to ensure that his family would never "bother him again" had struck Tom dumb.

"You know that there was no other way, Tom. In your heart, you know that it had to be done. I simply did what you did not have the courage to do."

Tom felt conflicted. He knew he should be angry, murderous even, given what Walter had done. But for reasons he did not fully understand, Tom could not even feel angry. He just felt weak. As though a great weight had been lifted from his shoulders but his entire body was still exhausted and needed rest.

Not knowing what else to say, Tom weakly replied, "Well, I thank you for helping me achieve my freedom. I am grateful. But tell me, why have you come here today?"

Walter, content that Tom had regained some composure, gestured to the seat across from him. Tom got up and then sat down across from Walter in a daze. He was still trying to wrap his mind around the information he had just been presented.

"You have achieved nothing, Tom. Though they are gone, your family still constricts your every thought and movement. Their images are burned into your mind."

Tom, visibly upset, muttered, "They're everywhere I go. Every face I see reminds me of them."

"What would you give to be free? How devoted are you really, Tom?"

"I'd give everything, anything. I just want to be able to stop thinking about them. I want to be free whatever it takes."

"Then so be it, it will be done."

Walter stood and carried his chair to the fireplace. He gestured to Tom to sit down in the chair. Tom, confused, questioned, "If you could free me so easily, why didn't you do it before?"

The Stranger Inside

Tom continued to follow Walter's demands, hoping to find some guidance.

Walter, grabbing his leather bag, replied, "You were not ready for your journey."

"Journey? What are you on about?" Tom said, as he situated himself in the new chair.

"You say you want freedom. Well, ultimate freedom is not a process. It is a journey that one must take. To embark, you must see physically all that your mind feels. Your mind and body must become one."

"That sounds like a lot of spiritual hoopla."

"In a sense, I guess it is. But there is no better way to explain the journey. Your mind is bound by the thoughts of your family. They haunt you and bind you even though they are gone. Your body must feel this as well to even have a chance at understanding," Walter said. Removing a rope from his bag, he added, "Though it may not be willing."

Walter walked over to Tom and tied him to the chair. Walter left Tom's hands free to move in his lap so as to not leave him too uncomfortable.

Tom, panicking, questioned Walter, "What are you doing!"

Walter calmly replied, "Freeing your mind from all constraints—from all responsibility."

Walter removed a single ornament from the previously forgotten Christmas tree looming in the corner. The ornament was a decorative picture frame engraved with "Our First Christmas" encasing a photograph of Tom's family.

"The image of your family is forever burned in your thoughts. This agony is compounded by the memories you created with your family and everything that represents them despite the fact that they are gone forever. In order to release your mind, your body must understand its pain."

The Stranger Inside

Walter removed the photo from the casing, took hold of the photo album Tom had originally armed himself with and reached for his leather bag. Walter then removed a Zippo lighter form the bag and set the picture and the photo album on fire, placing both burning objects at the base of the Christmas tree.

Finally escaping the shock of the situation, Tom screamed, "What are you doing?! How is that supposed to help?! Put that out!"

Walter replied, as if not to Tom but rather, to himself, "And they come to Jesus, and see him that was possessed with the devil, and had the legion, sitting, and clothed, and in his right mind; and they were afraid."

Walter then turned away from Tom, casually tossed the still lit Zippo lighter to one side, and began to walk away.

"What the hell! Are you completely insane?!" Tom cried out.

Walter stopped and turned back slightly, "I wish you the best of luck on your journey, Thomas. May the world look on to you with fear and admiration for your freedom."

Walter left the house just as the carpet began to catch fire.

The church tower down the street struck its midnight bells and ushered in the New Year. Thomas was finally a free man.

The Sitter

The Boys

The day was relatively unremarkable. It was September 25 and a Monday. Jack and Oliver had gone to school as expected, but they could not bear to sit still. They had been anticipating this day for too long and could hardly wait a minute more. Oliver was taking it much worse, he began to visualize their excursion vividly in his head. They would run out of the school past the town's library where they had been spending their afternoons researching the town's most famous tale, the legend of Uriel's Light. And finally down to the edge of town where they would be greeted with the overgrown monstrosity that was Wicker Forest. He couldn't get further in his fantasy due to the ringing of the class bell. It was lunch time and only one block remained for the boys. At lunch, their friends interrogated them about their endeavors just hoping to get a glimpse of what they were feeling.

One boy yelled to Jack from across the schoolyard, "You know you won't make it back J.J. It's like suicide walking that path!"

The boys were aware of the rumors; they had been studying each detail for weeks. The new kid seemed overly confused when he walked onto the schoolyard, as if they were all privy to some knowledge he was barred from. The new kid, hoping to alleviate his confusion, questioned Jack, "What path are you talking about?"

Oliver replied before Jack was given the opportunity, "Uriel's Light."

*   *   *

Uriel's Light

The Stranger Inside

In a small forgotten town out in the country, there were rumors of a man who once lived on the bluffs at the end of a path. The story would always change from person to person, though the structure was always the same. A man named Edgar who was bereaved at the loss of his wife had become a muted recluse. The town eventually thought the pain had killed him. He was too strong for that though. He had known, be it from an enigmatic voice within or just intuition, that his purpose had not yet been fulfilled. He would sit by his fire, day in and day out, through summer and winter, explaining every action in his life. The legend goes to say that one day, Edgar stopped thinking. He found the one decision that did not fit. Upon this realization, he threw the rest of his stock of wood into his fireplace. He ran from his house to the town to share the revelation but no one would listen. It was Sunday, and the town was at mass concentrating on the reverend's sermon. Admitting defeat, he retreated back on the path that led to his house. As his steps progressed, they slowed until he was stopped.

The forest was quiet except for a single voice. The voice emanated from the embers that marked his house's remains. Some say it was his wife that called for him, but some say it was Uriel himself answering Edgar's pleas for explanation. Whichever you believe, the voice he heard told him to go to the ledge, and he will see enlightenment for all that it is. Desperate for validation of his revelation, he ran there. Once Edgar looked down to the bottom of the bluff, he was carried off on the back of Uriel; Edgar was never seen again after that day.

The legend, however, continues to tell that under the harvest moon, you can see a small cloud of smoke originating over the spot where Edgar's house once stood. Any man who chooses to seek out the source of the smoke is led to the ledge. His mind is taken over by compulsion, and he is drawn to look out over the edge to see what Edgar saw. Most men that follow that smoke are never seen again, but the few that return are inimitably changed. They leave their families, they become deaf and blind. The world is too much for them. Unable to ever express what they had witnessed; whatever lies at the base of the bluffs was forever burned into their eyes.

* * *

The Meeting

The new kid asked Jack, "You guys must be crazy to try to find that path! Sure, it's just a myth but what do you really know about it?"

Jack and Oliver had done inordinate research to validate as many of the story's claims as they could. After weeks of deliberation, there was nothing about the legend that they could definitively refute. A man named Edgar did once live in their town, very much matching the description provided by more detailed accounts of the tale. The Edgar that they found had a wife whom he outlived in his home in the woods. And the last fact that they discerned was that a violent fire had erupted on the harvest moon several years after the recorded death of Edgar's wife. The boys had decided that this was ample evidence to substantiate a voyage into the once-forsaken forest surrounding their town.

Jack and Oliver looked at each other and harmoniously replied, "Enough."

Once school had finally recessed, the boys walked out ahead of the crowd. They began to walk faster out of excitement and ambition. Briskly walking past the familiar businesses and buildings that made up their meek city, Jack and Oliver eventually reached the edge of town.

Over the years since the origin of the story, the path had become overgrown. No one dared tread it, because they had heard the stories. The townsfolk were good, God-fearing men that sought no trouble from the likes of angels. They saw what happened to those men who dared walk the path as a punishment for trying to see what was not shown to them. The path had become so overrun with shrubs and growth that were it not for the rocks defining its edges, the boys would never have found it.

But after nearly a month of work and hours of devil-may-care careening through the woods, they were on their way. They had come prepared for this moment. Oliver removed a map and compass from his knapsack, and he and Jack began to study it. One problem they had not prepared for would hinder their momentum, but they would not realize their mistake until much later. But as it stood, they had not taken into consideration the bluffs themselves. The bluffs, located at the south of town, were enriched with iron deposits which the nearby mine had capitalized on. These deposits had thrown off their directions and sent them spiraling in the wrong direction. Heading heedlessly down the timid path, the boys were blissfully unaware that they were lost.

Wandering down the path, the boys grew tired. Ready to give in, Oliver put his bag down. Jack, however, did not see this; he was yards ahead and had come to a stop on his own. Noticing this sudden halt, Oliver grabbed his bag and ran to catch up to his friend. "What's the deal Jack?" No sooner had Oliver finished his question did he realize the cause of the restraint. They had reached a clearing. The boys had not seen an open space in over three hours, and it came as a shock. Convinced that they had found the spot where Edgar's house once stood, the boys began to celebrate. However, their delight was cut short by an overwhelming sense of paranoia. They felt some presence lingering over them and, without a word, felt the need to investigate. Fearful, the boys surveyed the clearing. Upon close examination they spotted the source of the feeling that consumed them. A woman sat precociously toward one side of the clearing; her legs were crossed and her arms rested on her lap. Jack, advancing cautiously, beckoned to her, "Hey lady, whatchya doin'?"

She did not respond.

"Didya hear me?" Jack insisted.

She did not react at all.

Jack, growing impatient, gestured to Oliver to come follow. The boys proceeded, slowly at first, until they were within feet of her. She sat, without expression, staring at the ground near their feet. Her hair fell down in front of her, almost touching her neatly crossed legs. She was morbidly skinny and as pale as a ghost. This sight was too much for Oliver to bear, and he began to retreat into the center of the clearing. Jack, as stubborn as he was impatient, waved his hands in front of her face. He yelled to her, "Hey, you, can you hear me? What's your name?" The lady coughed, as if in response.

This was enough for Jack, his stubbornness had broken, and he realized he was standing alone. However, before he could join his friend the Sitter lurched and grabbed hold of Jack's leg.

"Crederes angelus si loqueretur tibi?" she whispered before reclaiming her position.

Jack ran as fast as he could. He did not care that Oliver had not taken the hint to run as well. He was petrified and wanted to be home in his bed. Jack veered off the path, and luckily, Oliver had nearly caught up to see this deviation. The boys ran through the uncharted forest for what seemed like hours until they reached their town. Jack fell to the ground and began to shake. Oliver, trying to comfort his disheveled friend, rubbed his back and asked, "What did she say to you?"

Jack refused to speak; he was unwilling to divulge the reason for his state. Oliver, noticing the sun falling toward the horizon, stood Jack up and walked himself and Jack to their neighboring houses. As the two split ways, Oliver yelled to Jack, "Helluvah day we had, huh? See you in school tomorrow, man."

But Oliver did not see Jack in school the next day. No one except Jack's family saw him for the next few days. Jack had not said a word since the incident, but his silence was finally broken a few nights later at dinner. Jack had dazed off while eating his steak. Irritated by her motionless mute of a son, Jack's mother grabbed Jack's arm to put his steak back on the plate. Jack, before his mother could grasp his hand, slapped her away and screamed, "Don't touch me!" before running to his room. Jack's mother was fearful for her son but overjoyed at the fact that he spoke. She excused herself from the remaining family members at the table and proceeded toward her son's room. She slowly opened the door and realized her son was sitting in the center of the floor rocking back and forth. "Jack, honey, what is all this about? What happened to you?"

Jack began to speak, "In the forest on the outside of town, there's a woman. It was in a clearing deep in the middle of the forest, I think somewhere near the bluffs. She was just sitting there. She's all pale and ghostly it was weird. But Oliver and I found her, and I walked over to try to talk to her, and she wouldn't answer me. So I got closer, and then she grabbed me and said something in a weird language. It was really scary, and I just can't get the picture of her out of my head."

Jack's mother, noticeably concerned, began to question as to why he was there in the first place. Jack had not told his mother why he had been spending his afternoons in the library for so long, but the truth always comes out eventually. He spilled everything: the research, the plan, Uriel's Light, and even that they had stolen the compass. His mother was disappointed. "You are not to go back there again, under any circumstance. I'm going to call the police and tell them that you've been assaulted by some woman in the forest. This town can't afford to have a lunatic like that out there running around."

"You mean sitting," Jack quietly said.

"Yes, of course. Sleep tight, dear, you have school in the morning."

Friday morning, Jack's mother forced him to return to school. None of the kids bothered Jack. Their mothers were all called the night before and informed about his experience. The mothers were as sympathetic as possible, but no amount of sympathy could make Jack feel better about the situation.

* * *

The Reverend

A woman did, in fact, sit in the forest on the outskirts of town. Her age was of no importance to the townsfolk; they cared little for anomalies in their town. Of those who cared, no one knew whether she was even still a girl or a woman. She had been there for weeks but no one could really pinpoint when she had arrived there. During her time in the town, she had only spoken to Jack. As far as anyone was concerned she was barely a person at all. For this reason, the town named her as creatively as an animal: the Sitter. The Sitter had been doing just that since she was first spotted.

It became a running fad to go into the forest and try to talk to the Sitter. But she did not utter a word after her meeting with Jack. Groups of teenagers, kids, and adults alike wandered through the once-apostatized forest. Their attempts to break the Sitter's gaze all came to no avail. Though the general populace cared little for her presence, she was a main topic of conversation, especially on Sunday. The townsfolk had assembled for Sunday mass and were taking their seats in the church's pews. One man asked the reverend before he began his sermon, "What are we going to do about the Sitter?"

"That is not my place, Joseph, I am not the law—I am only a man of God. She is not sinning, and she is doing no wrong."

Joseph replied, "But we heard she grabbed your son and that he was the only one to hear her speak. Do you know what she said?"

"The rumors are true, my boy, and the O'Donnell's boy were the firsts to spot her. As well, she did grab him, but Jack could not remember what she said. He said it was another language. But folks, this is not the topic of today's sermon." The reverend tried to reconcile his audience and convene on the topics at hand.

After the mass had closed, Nathaniel, the town's reverend, locked the doors and headed toward the forest. He had heard enough of the rumors; he wanted to see her for himself.

*   *   *

The Sitter

Nathaniel followed what the rumors told and walked to the middle of the forest. Every step he took, the sky grew darker. But as it were, as the sky grew darker, the full moon grew brighter and rose higher in the sky. Nathaniel was fortunate he had chosen to venture out under the guidance of the Harvest Moon, for it is believed to be the brightest of moons. It grew colder as he walked but he found the clearing at last. Noticing the lady perched in her quiescent position, he began to approach her. He did not make it more than a few steps before her head jerked up toward him.

She beckoned to the reverend, "Crederes angelus si loqueretur tibi?"

"What does that mean?"

"Crederes angelus si loqueretur tibi!" she repeated.

"I don't understand what you're saying. I know that it's Latin, but what does it mean?"

The Sitter adjusted her position, and calmly stated, "Would you believe an angel if one spoke to you?"

"Well, of course, I would. Provided I knew that it was, in fact, an angel."

The Sitter reformed her position as Nathaniel questioned her, "Why would you ask such a thing, and why are you out here?"

"We both know why I'm out here, it's the same reason you're out here. It's the same reason you get up in the morning. It's the same reason you're still talking to me."

"And what exactly is that reason?"

"To get answers to questions we haven't asked yet," she said almost smugly.

"How can you know you've received the answer if you don't even know the question?"

"You're not really a reverend are you?"

"No, not legally. But the townsfolk believe in my words, and I enjoy helping them."

"So are you even a man of God at all?"

The Stranger Inside

"Well, yes, my family was raised very Christian. I just never went through the proper channels to become ordained. The town is so small that no one really cares too much for credentials. But, ma'am, back to you; why are you here in this spot?"

"I honestly could not tell you why I came here or how I got here. What I can tell you is that I cannot leave. I am forced with two options and a third I can create for myself provided I see it a fit solution."

Nathaniel sat down on the ground, preparing himself for a long conversation.

The Sitter gestured to her right, "Over here is a path, which a voice tells me to follow. And over to my left," gesturing to that direction, "is another less traveled path. The voice tells me to avoid this one. However, my third option is to walk the path that you came on, out of the forest entirely."

"I don't see where your problem lies ma'am. Why not just follow the voice? It must be from within if you're the only one to hear it."

"You hear your inner monologue daily, no doubt about that. However, when you hear a voice outside of your own, do you trust it? Can you honestly allow yourself to trust anything that does not come from within yourself?"

"Well yes, of course, that's where faith comes from. That's the entire premise of the idea of faith."

"Sure, you preach faith. But if someone came to you with a logical idea disproving a strong belief of yours, like God, you'd discount it. You only accept those ideas in which you'd think of yourself."

Nathaniel sat for a while contemplating the conversation. He had not expected such an exchange when he sat down.

"Why do you care if I would believe an angel?"

The Sitter started to seize slightly. She began to lose control over her bodily functions and her hands erupted wildly from her lap. After her hands, her arms soon followed. The rest of her body was not far behind when she started to foam at the mouth.

Recollecting herself, unknowing of what she just endured, she said, "Because, I hear one now."

Nathaniel, befuddled, leaned backward, trying to absorb what had just unfolded.

The Sitter continued, "He tells me which way to go. He tells me where that path will lead. But how can I believe him? How can I know where this voice truly comes from?"

"Only God knows the future, only God is omniscient and his angels are his messengers. So if the angels are speaking to you and telling you the future, then you should follow them."

"But isn't it I who has to interpret their message? How do I know they're trying to talk to me? How do I know that I'm not being tricked into some sort of self-fulfilled prophecy?"

"That is the secret of faith. That is the line between reason and insanity. If you choose to believe the voice, then you're sane; you have control, and you made a choice," the reverend said, hoping to end the conversation. He began to fear he would soon overstep his boundaries as a priest and begin to embark on to his personal ideas.

"Do you hear it too?"

"No, the angels must see something in you, something worth saving. You are indeed a lucky one. But there is one thing I don't understand, why you are sitting here?"

The Sitter stared at Nathaniel for nearly an eternity before replying, "I wanted to make a decision. I no longer wanted to just live; I wanted to choose to live."

"But I don't see why you chose . . ."

"Few people see it anymore, but this path forks." The Sitter interjected, "The right path is well known, I believe it is called Uriel's Light around here. However, the left path has been overgrown and forgotten for years, decades, centuries even. The left path leads to the train tracks, and those lead directly north. The issue I face is that the angel tells me to go right, so that he can talk to me more. There is something about that path that allows him to be heard more clearly."

"Then why not listen to him and take a leap of faith?"

"Because that is a leap I am not willing to risk."

Noticing the setting sun, Nathaniel admitted defeat, "Well, I'm sorry I could not be of more help to you, but it is getting late. My family must be worried about me."

Retreating back the way he came, Nathaniel became immobilized by the horizon. He saw out of the corner of his eye a most ominous sight—a single stream of smoke, billowing into the sunless sky. Without thought, he was overcome by the view and wanted nothing but to see its origin. Nathaniel stalked toward the smoke and toward the auspicious path. As Nathaniel began to trudge ever farther out of sight, the Sitter adjusted herself to watch her new acquaintance drift off into the distance.

Taken by a pitted fear for Nathaniel's safety, the Sitter began to try to stand. She had nearly forgotten what muscles did, what and how exactly coordination was supposed to work. After minutes of deliberation and exertion, she was on her feet shuffling after her friend.

Once the clearing was vacant, Jack and Oliver appeared from their hiding places. Without words, they agreed to follow the Sitter and Jack's father down the path.

* * *

The Sitter reached the end of the path and the origin of the smoke. There was no clearing where a house used to be. There was no clearing at all. The path led straight to the bluffs. The path led straight to Nathaniel, starring into what lay beneath the bluffs—where the smoke originated.

As the Sitter reached the bluff, she too was drawn to the cliff. The voice grew louder and louder as she neared the edge. He kept screaming to her as she stared into the horizon. She could no longer take it. Drawing a rock from the ground, the Sitter began to bludgeon her ears with all her might in hopes to end the sound. No matter what she did, it was to no avail.

Her ears were bleeding as she fell to the ground and crawled toward the brink. The boys arrived as she began to cry, and they trudged along to stand next to Nathaniel. In unison, they all took a single step.

They took their leap of faith as the Sitter finally peered over the edge. Watching the bodies career lifelessly toward the bluff, she screamed and felt her throat closing in. She grabbed another rock from the limitless pile and began to blind herself. Strike after strike caused tears of red to pour down her face. Her skin was stained with blood as the voice grew to be overpowering. With all her strength she rose to her feet. Gasping for air, she screamed to the heavens, "I will not jump!"

The Guardians

It's raining again, and the sky is gray and overcast. But then, that's nothing out of the ordinary in a London winter. It's a rare moment when you catch a bit of blue sky peeking out of the cloud cover at this time of year. I like it when there's a bit of blue sky round about the clouds. Always looks pleasant, reminds me of spring a bit. Could use a bit of springtime feeling right now, this place feels like a dirty hospital, and I don't like it at all.

I don't know if they will ever let me go, after what I saw. I don't know if they will ever actually answer my questions either. They probably won't. Damned quiet bastards they are. I know I'm still in London, the weather I can see out my one window can tell me that much at least. Can't really see down below the window though, there's some sort of rooftop ledge in the way. I think this room is near one of the above grounds through. Sometimes I swear I can hear the train going by. Maybe it's my imagination, who knows. Hard for me to say I know anything anymore.

I only know one thing for certain at this point—that is, what I saw happen was real. You know when something's real, you can feel it in your bones. And what I saw was real. Real in a frightening way. Though, I actually do know more than just one thing. I know that those three men are not letting me go anytime soon; I imagine they're still fussing over what to do with me.

They frighten me, those men. Unnerved me when they first came to my desk that day when they were looking for George. They have an eerie kind of feel to them, like they have business to take care of, and they intend to take care of it any which way they have to. Their eyes were strange as well. Gray. All three of them had the same gray eyes. A bit odd, I thought at the time.

The Stranger Inside

I just want to go home. Never thought I'd ever miss my little place in Greenwich so much. I just want to go home and try to forget about this whole mess. Maybe go to the pub, get a pint, and try to relax. But I guess that's not really an option right now, is it? The Guardians won't let me go.

*   *   *

It was just before midday when three tall men walked toward the Barclay Bank building in Canary Wharf. They had been given orders to carry out a mission, a mission of most grave import. They had to find George Leery.

George was an accountant, working in the bank for almost a year. George was well liked by his colleagues and no one had an unkind word to say about him. This was mostly due to the fact that no one really knew anything about him at all. Everyone knew he was a kind man, not prone to fits of emotion. Everyone knew he always came to work precisely ten minutes early so he could fix himself a coffee before starting work. Everyone knew that George was a hard worker and would help anyone else in the department if they were falling behind. Everyone could tell you that his favorite sandwich was salt beef with a bit of English mustard and that, on Wednesdays, he liked having leek and potato soup with his sandwich. These few tidbits of information, however, were the most that anyone knew about George Leery. It didn't bother anyone that no one knew much about him though. He did appear rather ordinary after all.

Michael Durn, one of the security guards who minded the Barclay's doors was the only person who talked to George on a consistent basis. Michael and George took lunch at quarter past noon and both had an affinity for salt beef, and so a small friendship was made. Michael liked talking to George because George didn't make Michael feel uneducated, though in truth he *was* rather uneducated. George liked talking to Michael because Michael was a simple man who didn't ask many personal questions and preferred talking of such things as the weather or the latest rugby match.

It was on a Thursday just before midday. George was getting ready to take lunch with Michael when three men with gray eyes were walking toward the Barclay Bank building in Canary Wharf.

As the three men with gray eyes entered the building, Michael was just preparing to go to the break room to take his lunch with George. Upon seeing the three visitors, Michael looked around for Ben, the security guard who did the walking rounds and usually covered for Michael during his breaks. Unable to spy Ben, Michael reluctantly put his lunch back down on the desk and greeted the three men who were now before him.

"Morning, gents, what can I do for you?"

The tallest man spoke, in a low voice that seemed to echo, "We search for the man you call George Leery."

"You got business with him then? He expecting you?"

"He has been expecting us for a very long time."

"Ah, been running late, have you? Don't worry, George is a patient fellow, I'm sure he won't begrudge you for making him wait. Lucky for you I'm about to head over to the break room to have my lunch with George right now, as a matter of fact. I can tell him you're here if it's a pressing matter. Or perhaps you'd rather I show you to him then?"

The tallest man turned first to his right and then to his left, as though communicating something with the other men standing beside him. He then turned back to George.

"Lead us to him."

"All right, lads, follow me," Michael said, picking up his lunch from the desk and gesturing for the three men to follow. Michael was quite willing to breach security protocol, just this once, and take the men to the break room. He was rather hungry after all.

The Stranger Inside

Perhaps though, Michael would not have been so willing to lead the three men to George had he noticed that upon their entrance into the bank, the sky had visibly darkened and the flowers in the pots by the door had turned as gray as the men's eyes.

"So you lads business associates of George's then? Some number-crunching work to be done for the bank or some such?"

The man who had spoken before said, "We are keepers of the order, and the man who you call George Leery has diverted from the path that was given to him."

Michael, not really understanding what was being said to him but not wanting to feel out of place, replied, "All right, I gotcha."

Walking now in silence, Michael began to feel more and more uncomfortable. The men appeared to be rather official and seemed to have some important business with George, but something felt off in their demeanor. Michael couldn't quite place why he felt this way, but the fact remained that he suddenly would have much rather not had to deal with these three gray-eyed men.

After another few minutes of thick, walking silence Michael turned to the three men.

"Right, lads, here we are. Just give me a minute to see if George is in here or if he's still in his office. Be just a moment."

Michael opened the door and walked into the break room, leaving the three gray-eyed men outside the door.

"Hello there, Michael, what have you got for lunch today?"

"Hey, George, and I think you well know. It is Thursday after all."

"Ah, spiced prawns and mayonnaise then, I presume?"

"Right you are, old boy, right you are. Got a bag of crisps as well," said Michael, smiling.

"Take a seat, Michael," George said, gesturing to the chair next to him.

"I would, George, I would. But first there's a pinch of business to clear up, see, there's these three blokes just outside said they got business with you. It seems you been expecting them awhile, so I figured if it was real urgent you wouldn't mind me bringing them up here."

George looked back at Michael, an expression of puzzlement upon his face. "I think there's been some mistake, Michael. I'm not expecting anyone at the present."

Michael's brow furrowed, and he opened his mouth to speak, but before he could, the break room door behind him opened, and the three gray-eyed men walked in.

"There is no mistake except on your part for thinking that we would not find you," spoke the tallest of three.

At the sight of the three men, a cloud passed over George's face, his eyes darkened, and he frowned deeply.

"Hey now, what's all this then?"

Michael's query remained unanswered.

"I suppose it was only a matter of time," George said, slowly lifting up his head to meet the gaze of the three gray-eyed men.

The tallest replied, "You have always known that this day would come. You could not forever run from the purpose the Master gave to you."

"You mean the purpose he tried to force upon me."

"It was given to you and you departed from it, and so mankind was forced to suffer for your selfishness."

"It was his purpose, not mine!" exclaimed George, jumping up out of his chair, fists clenched.

Michael found himself completely dumbstruck. Seeing the usually placid George in such a state had a seemingly paralytic effect on him.

"It was the purpose given to you by the Master so that his children would be led to salvation."

"And what of my purpose? What of my salvation?" George practically screamed back at the tallest of the three men.

The Stranger Inside

"Your salvation lies in the fulfillment of the purpose given to you by the Master."

Silence.

Michael still stood, open-mouthed, looking back and forth between the three men and George.

"So," George said, still looking defiantly at the three gray-eyed men, "I suppose he sent you three to come find me."

"We are the Guardians. We serve and protect the one who the Master created to bring his children to salvation."

"I see. So you are here to force me to my purpose, is that it?"

"No."

George took a step back in surprise.

"What?"

"We are the Guardians. We serve and protect the one who the Master created to bring his children to salvation. And you are no longer the one we serve. You are no longer the one we protect."

At these words the three men advanced a few paces toward George.

"What?" George cried. "What are you saying? You can't possibly mean what you say!"

"Since you would not serve the Master's design, the Master has created another. One who shall fulfill his purpose and lead the Master's children to salvation. The one we now serve only requires a vessel and then the work shall begin."

The three gray-eyed men continued to advance toward George.

"Get back! Get away from me! Michael, help me!"

George's cry for help roused Michael from his trancelike state. Realizing his friend was in danger, he rushed toward the three men, only to be suddenly blinded by a white light and feel himself falling. When Michael's vision cleared, he found himself on the floor in the exact spot he had just been standing.

"Please stop! You don't have to do this!" George pleaded, falling now on his knees.

The Stranger Inside

"We are the Guardians. We serve and protect the one who the Master created to bring his children to salvation. And you, the Master's disobedient son, pose a very grave danger to the one whom we now serve. "

The three gray-eyed men stood now before the prostrate George. Michael, still lying on the floor and unable to get up, stared hopelessly at his now weeping friend

The three gray-eyed men, looking down upon George, all raised their right hands.

"NO!"

Spoken in unison, "As God wills it, so it shall be."

From the hands of the three men erupted a white light. Michael watched as the light surrounded George and, as George screamed, entered his body through his eyes and mouth. A smell of sulfur suddenly suffused the air. Michael watched as George's body slowly melted into a pool of steaming yellow liquid.

The three gray-eyed men lowered their hands, the white light dimmed, and they took three steps away from the slowly receding puddle that was once George.

"How? How could you do that? That's impossible!" panted Michael as he stared up into the eyes of the three men who now stood around him.

"What shall we do with him?"

"He isn't dangerous, perhaps we should leave him?"

"No," spoke the tallest of the three gray-eyed men, "We shall not leave him here, the Master may have use for him. We shall take him with us."

Suddenly, Michael's vision went black.

* * *

The Stranger Inside

It was raining, and Michael was looking up at the sky through the one window in the room where the three gray-eyed men had been keeping him, when the door opened and his captors walked in. Seeing the three men, Michael got up and placed himself before them.

"Now, you listen here, and you listen good," Michael began, intent on having his say. "If you plan on doing me in, then I suggest you do it now. I'm tired of waiting here and not knowing what's on and what's not. So do your worst now, if you please."

Michael stood squarely, chest out and breathing deep, facing his captors.

The tallest of the three men stepped forward, "Fear not. The time for waiting is at an end."

At these words, the three gray-eyed men each raised their right hands. Michael did not move.

Nor did he cry out for mercy.

Nor did he weep on his knees.

He simply stood.

Spoken in unison, "As God wills it, so it shall be."

From the hands of the three men erupted a white light.

* * *

In the room that once held Michael Durn, there was a pervasive smell of honeysuckle. The rain outside had also stopped, and there was a break in the dark cloud cover that let a few stray beams of light sneak past the gloom to kiss the earth.

The three gray-eyed men, heads bowed in obeisance, were now kneeling before the vessel they had prepared for their Master's creation.

In the body that once held Michael Durn now resided the one who would lead the Master's children to salvation. The Savior slowly rose to his feet, testing the body that had been emptied for him, testing his physical strength. He then turned and looked out of the window at the sunlight that had snuck past the clouds and carried him down from the heavens.

"My brother could not fulfill his purpose, and so my father's earthly children were left to damnation," spoke the Savior. "Now I must correct the mistakes made by my brother."

"We are the Guardians. We serve and protect the one who the Master created to bring his children to salvation."

The Savior looked at his faithful servants and smiled. "The time for waiting is at an end. Now, we shall give my father's children salvation. Now, we shall begin the purification by fire."

Spoken in unison, "As God wills it, so it shall be."

Searching for Gethsemane

* * *

The thoughts of Judgment awaken
bring me closer to my calling.
The losses pile effortlessly
climbing toward the ceiling.
A forgotten voice from years before
creeps forevermore into my pen
haunts my every thought
and hinders every motion.
The burning of her love
unbridled and wholly free.
He strikes me down with blank stares
and opens up this Pandora's box.
She is torn apart by her heart
and leaves her only son.

* * *

It can be said that a man's surroundings will often reflect the man. Such was the case for Noah. Noah Thompson's apartment was, to those few people who ever saw it and especially to her, a rather accurate reflection of his character. It is not all that surprising then that soon after the incident that took place on December 31, both Noah and his little apartment were forgotten.

The Stranger Inside

The building Noah lived in was relatively new compared to the other buildings of the neighborhood, and yet, despite the building's young age, it seemed worn beyond its years. The sidewalk in front of the entrance to the building was cracked and in need of repair. The three concrete steps leading up to the door were under assault from a number of very persistent weeds. If you were to walk through the once white but now graying doorway, you would see a faux mahogany staircase hugging the left wall. To the right of the staircase, a small dark green couch silently sat sentinel along the right wall before the entrance to a small hallway leading to the landlord's residence. Why that couch rested there no one ever knew. The entire inside of the entrance is dimly lit by an old, shabby, but everlastingly functional chandelier hanging from the ceiling.

The staircase leads to one of two floors. The second floor was home to an elderly man by the name of Mr. Greaves. He was an old man simply waiting to die. His wife had passed away nearly a decade before, and upon her passing, Mr. Greaves found himself alone in a rapidly changing world he did not quite understand. He soon sold the house where he and his wife had lived and moved into the apartment below Noah. He rarely left. Besides the necessary grocery shopping and trips to the liquor store, Mr. Greaves was hardly ever seen. Not that this disturbed his landlord, for his rent checks were always on time.

If you continued up the staircase past the landing in front of Mr. Greaves's rooms, you would find yourself on the third floor of the rapidly aging building. At the top of the staircase, you are greeted by a small landing with the door to Noah's apartment on your right side. If you chose to walk past his door, you would be able to look out of a small dirty window into the street below. No one ever did this. There was nothing to see really.

Noah's apartment was simple. Open his door and you would be confronted with a hallway that gave the impression that to walk through it would require you to hunch over slightly, though this was not actually necessary. This hallway was no more than a few feet in length and quickly deposited you at the threshold of a small living room. It was here that Noah spent much of his time. Despite that though, there really wasn't much there. Looking into the living room from the hallway you see the back of a cheap couch facing a TV placed in the corner like some altar to apathy. Against the right wall of the living room sat the desk where Noah wrote the poetry that was eventually published in his first small book. There wasn't much on the desk besides a few scraps of paper and a copy of the little book he had finally gotten published. That book was Noah's pride and joy. After its publication a year ago, however, Noah had yet to hand his next manuscript in to his publisher. His publisher didn't seem to care all that much. To the right of the desk is a doorway that leads to a dirty little kitchen that barely functioned. Noah used the oven space as an extra cabinet, since the oven itself was useless. The stovetop was always dirty despite the fact that Noah did not cook often. He preferred to take his meals at the Café Noir down the street. If he had to make a meal for himself, it generally consisted of nothing more that some beans, a sausage, a few pieces of toast, and some tea all washed down with cheap gin. Had you gone past the desk instead of turning into the kitchen, you would have entered Noah's spartan bedroom. A bed, a dresser, some scattered clothes, a small nightstand with a digital clock, and a broken mirror was all you would see. There was little else.

* * *

My notes are how I speak my mind,
and how I get things done.
They tell the story I dare not say,
from that I'll always run.
The pain of how you tell me what,
I must never dream or do.
The stories that you told to me,

The Stranger Inside

the tales that I'd soon rue.
I'll never speak the words I write,
nor will you ever see their ink.
You'll never know just how I feel,
or even what I think.
I'll shut you out in notes I write,
and drown you with my tears.
The thing that pains the most,
is that you embody all my fears.
And so, I'll write down the words,
so my thoughts will stay deep inside.
And no one will know they're mine,
for these words I can't confide.
I will do everything just to spite you,
it's the final straw and my cards are read.
The thoughts you force on me,
continue to haunt me in my bed.
The things that you do to me,
will fill me up with rage,
It's not my concern to act on them,
so I'll dump them on the page.
The ink fills each and every line,
the whiteness fades away.
And still I put down more and more,
until I'm out of things to say.

* * *

I was taking my dinner today at the Café Noir, just like I usually do when something rather interesting made an impression on me. It was a young man sitting in the table in front of mine. His back was to me, and so he could not have had any way of knowing that I was observing him. He was clearly not supposed to be in the café. He would take a moment to glance around at the people in the café as though he were looking for someone. Then he would glance at his watch and frown. After nearly half of an hour, he gathered up his coat and walked up to the manager, Enrique, and asked what café he was in. Enrique told him he was in the Café Noir and the young man sighed and walked out of the café, frowning the whole while. As he was walking to the door, I heard him mutter something about being in the wrong place. He had clearly made some error and had come to the Café Noir during the time when I normally took dinner by mistake.

The young man I saw made a great impression on me. He seemed so lost and yet so oblivious at first to the fact that he had no idea where he was. I mean this literally as well as figuratively for the poor bugger really thought he was in a different café, a different restaurant. He was in the wrong place waiting for someone he may now never meet because he was in the wrong place and didn't even know it. He couldn't even correct his mistake because all the while he was unaware of the fact that he was making a mistake while he was sitting in the table in front of me.

If his body was in the Café Noir, but his being was meant to be elsewhere (with his unknown rendezvous in some other hole in the wall eatery), where was he? Was he really there in that café when I watched him, even though his essence was perhaps not meant to be there? Or was it meant to be there? Was it his body that got the right memo but accidentally left his soul behind? Where was he really supposed to be? Can a person lose their soul in this world while still living? It seems so to me. Look at all these people walking around, dazed and oblivious to their plight. Oblivious to the fact that they have lost the one thing that makes us truly great, truly human. These fools let the world distract them, and now they have lost their souls.

It reminds me of father. After the passing, he didn't know where he was supposed to be. Lost in a haze of cigarette smoke, photo albums, whiskey, and daytime television he forgot where he was. I remember staring into his eyes and asking him if I could have fifteen dollars to go out. He just looked at me with an empty sadness, like he didn't even know who I was. He wordlessly gave me the fifteen dollars and then went back to forgetting himself in his memories. I guess his spirit was always with mother the whole time. His body just got left behind I suppose.

I still think that was weakness. I cannot live like my father and suddenly become an inanimate object not even worthy of existence because I got lost, because I misplaced my soul. I refuse to simply exist. What is there in simply existing? What is there in being nothing more than a lampshade for the rest of my life?

I am Noah Thompson. I am not a lampshade. I am better than that.

* * *

and as I sit here, watching myself.
I wonder, will it ever come back?
extension from myself, I rarely,
if ever, seem to notice.
the sensation overwhelms,
the change in tone,
the change in tense,

the newly realized mood,

the ostentatious aura.

dissociative in a sense,

a world above another.

a racemic world,

one you can't get used to.

loss of time and balance,

association with your sight.

and yet pure and serene.

do you really want it back?

* * *

There is a distinct smell of burnt smoke coming from Noah's apartment.

Sitting up at two o'clock in the morning, Noah was struck by the urge to make himself some sausage. Naturally, this urge was followed by the urge to take a little drink, a little drink that soon turned into a big drink. It was precisely this big drink that then caused Noah to become lost in thought and forget to tend to the sausage he had set cooking upon his stove.

Suddenly, the smell caught his attention and he flew into action, quickly moving the pan onto some dirty dishes piled upon a sink whose bottom has rarely been seen. The smoke itself soon dissipates but the smell lingers. Noah stops and stares at the blackened pan he has set upon his dirty dishes. With the urge gone, he is wondering why he had set the sausage cooking in the first place.

This has become a daily ritual. Not the specific event of burning the sausage, although his absent-mindedness has led to culinary mishaps on more than one occasion, but a certain thoughtlessness that is practically ever present in Noah's life. Even in those set rituals that occur on an everyday basis, like his taking meals at the Café Noir, a constant daze followed Noah about. It was not that he was daydreaming, but rather he seemed to forget what it was he was looking at. One moment, he would be looking out the window of the café at people passing by, and the next moment, he would forget himself and no longer be conscious of what it was he was looking at. He did not replace the world he was forgetting with any other image, he simply forgot it. It was exactly this forgetful daze that further solidified his isolation from other people. He often did not even notice the fact that he had stopped taking notice of the word around him. To catch Noah's attention required a person to step into Noah's world, and Noah's world consisted of little but himself. Himself and the pungent smell of burning sausage.

* * *

Everything comes alive at night
My heart which beats faster for its very thought
The biggest fears are realized
My brain which constructs them into being
All your pain is washed away
My voice which speaks them on unwilling ears
The smallest light is brilliant
My eyes can feel their slightest glow
Happiness's only saving grace
My hands that force concealment
Entrance to the deepest depths
My feet that make me run and flee
Trapped between the sea of day
My body is bound in chains.

* * *

The Stranger Inside

I was walking down the street coming back from the Café Noir last night when I was struck by the urge to take the side street two blocks before my apartment building. Why the urge struck me I really cannot say, but I didn't question it at the time. These thoughtless urges strike me at random often enough that they are nothing to wonder at. Most of the time, if the urge does not seem too unreasonable, I will simply comply.

While walking down this dirty little street, I happened upon a couple walking down the opposite side of the lane, holding hands. They were like some picturesque Hallmark image of a happy couple. She, in her orange scarf, was all smiles and bubbly merriment looking up at him and feeling utterly secure. He, in his gray overcoat, was looking back with a proud smile almost as if he were saying to himself, "This is the love of my life, and with her I will always be happy."

For whatever reason, this sight made me disgusted, and not with the couple, but with myself. I have been wondering why I felt so disgusted and am having some difficulty in coming up with an answer. Am I jealous? I suppose I have to admit to that being a possibility. I have always thought myself better than most people and being above such pettiness, but I will at least allow the possibility of a momentary lapse in my reason. Granted, I am living alone at the moment and have been living alone for a rather large span of time now. But I have never felt the need to fill myself up with some other person. I have always viewed my self-imposed isolation as a sign of strength. I can't stand most people. A far as I am concerned, most people fall into four categories: pathetic cowards like my father or Mr. Greaves who cling to things that are not worth clinging to, arrogant bastards who think themselves so superior to me when in reality they don't have a clue about life, clingy weaklings who feel that without latching themselves onto somebody, they are unfulfilled and worthless, or people like me who are none of these things. There aren't very many people like me.

I don't think I was jealous of him for having that girl on his arm. But then again, I cannot explain my feeling of disgust that seemed to stem from myself either. No matter, that couple means nothing to me.

* * *

The opening to beyond,
a place you'll never go.
A place you couldn't dream of,
one you wouldn't want to.
It lies beneath the rubble,
from centuries long before.
Hidden from plain sight,
so no one will ever go.
Full of the unknown,
things that haunt most dreams.
They will make you crazy.
fill your thoughts with hate.
It's a place I lock and bolt,
a place you'll never find.
You'll search and search,
looking for years and years.

The Stranger Inside

But I can't help you search,

For I am looking too.

*　　*　　*

Noah enjoyed taking walks very much. He took at least one lengthy walk every day. On certain occasions, he would take more than one if the walking mood should strike him strongly again. Of the many moods that could strike Noah, his walking mood was by far his most pleasant. He would suddenly be struck with a mild sort of wanderlust and would put on a jacket and take to the streets. Walking had a calming effect on Noah most of the time. He would walk around and take in the sights about him. Whether or not these sights were something new to Noah was immaterial, for they would always receive equal attention. At least initially. After a time, of course, Noah would drift into his idle forgetfulness, and the world around him would slip away and he would see practically nothing.

The city neighborhood in which Noah lived was rather conducive to his long, ambling, and semicircuitous walks. It was a quiet neighborhood a little off the beaten path of the city. Its streets never found themselves overly crowded or busy, for you would not be in this neighborhood unless you had an express purpose in being there. It was by no means well-to-do, but it was not dangerous either, though if one should venture six or seven blocks south, the surroundings would become decidedly less friendly. You could often encounter young children at play during the afternoon, making a great deal of noise in their childish play. Noah liked listening to the children. They always seemed to be effortlessly happy to him.

Much of the inspiration for Noah's poetry would come from the things he saw on his walks and how they affected him—a girl walking by, the rustling sound of leaves, an overcast sky above the street. All these things would affect Noah in a different way, and in affecting him, would give his poetry new fodder.

One Tuesday afternoon, Noah was walking down the dimly illuminated stairway in his building with the intention of taking a walk when he came across Mr. Greaves standing on the second floor landing. The old man stood directly in the stairwell, blocking Noah's path. Had he not been blocking the way, Noah would scarcely have noticed Mr. Greaves at all. The old man was clearly drunk.

Mr. Greaves was wearing a pair of faded blue khakis and a yellowing dress shirt, once white, underneath a black sweater. His hands were veiny and prone to shaking, as they were at this moment. With his left hand, Mr. Greaves was tightly gripping the top of the stairwell's railing while his right hand was held up before his face and was trembling as though trying to grasp at something that wasn't there. His glasses were slightly askew, and the skin around the old man's bloodshot eyes was red from all the liquor he must have been drinking. His eyes were watery. Noah, of course, facing Mr. Greaves's back, could see nothing but an old man blocking his way downstairs.

After waiting for a few moments, Noah cleared his throat and spoke.

"Mr. Greaves, could you please move; you are blocking the way."

Turning around, allowing Noah to behold his weepy and inebriated visage, the old man stared hard and angrily into Noah's face. Noah had not expected such a reaction and was slightly taken aback. He opened his mouth, as if to say something to the old man, but stopped.

"You got somewhere to go, boy?" Mr. Greaves managed to wheeze out, "Got some big important appointment I'm making you late for?"

"No, I was going to take a walk."

"Oh! Well pardon me for momentarily delaying your walk in my distress, you self-conceited bastard."

"Mr. Greaves, I didn't mean . . ."

The Stranger Inside

"Oh shut it." Mr. Greaves cut Noah off, "I've heard enough from you. From everyone. Not a damn one of you cares what I think. But then why should you? I'm just an old drunkard living alone in a broken down building blocking everybody's way."

Mr. Greaves violently pushed himself away from the banister and stumbled over to his door. Placing both hands upon the door frame, he sobbed out a heavy and angry sigh. Noah was rooted to the spot. This was the longest exchange he had ever had with Mr. Greaves, and it was starting to frighten him, the man had been nothing but politely deferent on all previous occasions. The old man heaved a few more sobbing sighs, lifted his head, and turned to look back at Noah. His face had lost all traces of anger and now seemed almost pleading. A tear trickled down the old man's face.

"You don't understand what it's like, boy. You don't understand what it's like to have nothing and not be able to let go."

Mr. Greaves then turned back toward his door, his arms falling to his sides. With a listless motion, he opened his door and slowly walked inside, shutting the door behind him.

Noah was not sure what to do at first. Shaking his head and gathering himself, he walked down the rest of the stairs and out of the front door of his building. Noah looked around. The sky was a light blue and was peppered with a few small puffy clouds. He could hear some children running around in the distance and was buffeted by a cool breeze. Turning around, Noah looked back up at his building. Shaking his head, Noah set off down the street.

"Poor old man's a crazy fool," he muttered to himself.

* * *

Hold on till tomorrow,

you don't know what it will bring.

90

The Stranger Inside

Hold on to the dreams,
let them out so they can sing.
The days are numbered,
they are low but always there.
The past is forever gone,
the thoughts it holds are bare.
Lives on through the memories,
the thoughts that keep it holding on.
The dreams you held are on the run,
quick before they have long-since gone.

* * *

I am sitting in the park by the square about four or five blocks away from my house. Everything around me should cause me nothing but the greatest pleasure. It's just the right temperature so that I can walk about pleasantly in my light jacket. The bench I am sitting on is comfortable and painted in a light green color that I find quite lovely. There is a warbler singing in the trees and some doves resting on the bench opposite me. I can hear, but not see, the fountain in the center of the small park. Reminiscent of a small gurgling brook by my grandmother's house. There is one thing, however, that is tormenting me and destroying the entire scene. It is a color. Orange.

Normally, this autumn color does not bother me but right now there is one small patch of leaves on the tree beside my bench that is an absolutely abhorrent orange color. Just looking at it makes me angry. I feel ready to quarrel with anyone that walks by. Just now an elderly man tipped his hat to me as he passed me, I could have flown into a rage. I wanted to hit him.

The Stranger Inside

This is not normal for me. I hardly ever give in to such blind passions. It is out of character for me. It is giving in to such passion that makes a man weak. I am glad to have my notebook with me. Writing this all down helps me keep a calmer demeanor. I must go now. This park with its orange leaves is not a place for me to stay. I will go to the bar next to Café Noir, have a stiff drink, and then go to the café and take my lunch at the usual hour. Perhaps that will help to get this aggravating orange color out of my mind.

*   *   *

The words are written,
on the brim of your hat.
Be careful to whom you reveal it,
Your action will define you.
Think carefully before the act,
though the thought holds no steam.
The action of thought is not sure,
for you'll always change your mind.
Do not act with haste,
or in your own self-interest.
For the thoughtless action burns your heart,
and will relish in your deep subconscious.
The actions best suited
pull toward a new world order.
A brim that will soon express,
an action requiring no thought.
He writes these words with hidden intent;
To find the feelings meant for him.

The Stranger Inside

The ones that never were expressed,

the ones they would always deny.

You may know the truth,

but be unable to accept its very self.

The incarnation of all you thought,

will haunt you perched upon its shelf.

For action proves its holy worth

With each and every implement.

*   *   *

It was particularly dreary in Noah's apartment one late afternoon when Noah decided that he would take his dinner a little earlier than usual at the Café Noir. It was his faucet which was the catalyst for this rather unusual break in routine. Noah had attempted to stop the faucet's dripping several times before simply giving up. It became more and more irritating for him to hear it dripping, however, and prevented him from being able to concentrate on his work. It was because of this dripping faucet that Noah decided to take his dinner a little earlier than usual and bring his work with him to the Café Noir. Little did Noah know that this chance decision would change his life forever.

Picking up his light jacket and a manila folder with his manuscripts and his book within, Noah set out for the Café Noir. It was a cold day, and Noah instantly regretted not having brought his heavier jacket. With his manila folder tucked under his arm he shoved both hands as far into his pockets as possible and briskly walked to the Café.

Enrique greeted Noah as he walked in.

"Noah! Good to see you, my friend. It's a little early for you tonight, isn't it?"

"Just a little. I thought I'd come and do some work during dinner. My faucet was driving me mad."

93

The Stranger Inside

"Well, your usual table is ready as always. The usual, I gather?"

"Yes. Thanks, Enrique."

Noah sat down at his table and opened up the manila folder and surveyed its contents. It was a habit of his to examine each paper in his portfolio, despite already knowing what lay on each paper. After a few moments of careful survey, each paper was then placed in a pile according to which pieces Noah wanted to work on. It was during this cursory examination of his manuscripts that a young girl happened to walk by a little too closely to Noah's table, causing his manuscripts and his book to fall onto the floor when she brushed past them.

"Oh! I am so sorry, sir, let me help you with those."

She quickly stoops over to help Noah retrieve his materials and suddenly takes notice of the picture on the back cover of Noah's book. She freezes and stares back at Noah in wonder and astonishment.

"Oh my god, you're Noah Thompson!"

"Well, yes, I am." Noah is taken aback. Being recognized has startled him.

"I am such a fan of your work! I have read and reread your book so many times! I can't believe I'm actually meeting you in person!"

And so began the conversation that would change Noah forever.

*　　*　　*

She sits there staring off,
not knowing the difference she makes.
A careless gaze forthcoming
sets the tone of his stoic life
cracks the shell he built
but she doesn't even see him.
Her eyes rest on city signs
warning her of days to come.

The Stranger Inside

Though he's seen her before
this time breaks his very soul.
A dying breed of love
torn down from dreams of angels.
He'd sell his soul for one quick glance
a proof she feels the way he does.
Though the moment lasts forever
she leaves him in that primordial dust
to fend for himself
and prove it was never even real.
She too writes on her page
filling it with love and lust.
Passion is her downfall
it brings her to his level.
Hoping she will look and see
he writes her sonnets he will never speak.
A broken dream unrealized
crashes through the tattered ceiling tiles
sharing with her the life he lives,
overcoming the walls she'll use to block him out.

* * *

My heart is racing. God, how long it has been since someone has ever set my heart racing so. God how I never thought I would ever utter those words.

By what grand coincidence is it that we met? Who could say for what reason I chose to take my dinner at the Café Noir a little bit earlier on that day? Who can say for what reason I chose to bring my book and manuscripts with me so as to do some work at the café?

95

The Stranger Inside

Who can say why she chose to have her dinner at the very same café and take a table just behind mine? What were the chances she would accidentally knock some of my papers off my table and, in doing so, apologetically help me pick up the papers, thus revealing my book? What were the chances she then took note of the content of my manuscripts and recognize me from the back cover of my book? What were the chances that she was one of my readers?

I had known of course that after it's being published, my book of poetry would be read by people I didn't know, but to actually meet a reader and avid fan in person was a completely different matter.

Of course then she sits down, enamored with meeting me herself, and what a discussion that follows. What an exchange of thoughts that occurs between us! Such a stimulating conversation I have not had in so long I had practically forgotten what it was like. I am enchanted by her. I think that she may actually be enchanted with me. Such words of sincere praise for my work from her, and such hopeful expectation that I would soon publish more. It gladdened my heart to hear it.

I find my hands shaking as I write these words. Incredible. She affected me so greatly. I am seeing her again tomorrow. I told her that the Café Noir was my favorite place to take lunch and dinner and that I was there often. Of course, Enrique chimes in and tells her that I am his most loyal customer, and in fact, he could set his clocks by my arrival. She seemed delighted to hear this. She then proceeds to tell me that she lives nearby herself and hopes very much to see me again. I am excited beyond words. These words I write now become more and more illegible. I must put down my pen for a moment and pour myself some gin and tonic. It should steady me.

The Stranger Inside

A chance meeting with a beautiful girl. A beautiful girl who adores my work. A beautiful girl who (dare I put it in words?) adores me. A beautiful girl who I will be seeing again very soon. I can hardly believe it.

* * *

You stand there solemnly
with your one track mind intact.
Refuse to believe the words,
that come from me for no reason.
The multi-path will free you,
let you see you for all you are.
The paths will intertwine to one,
to make it easy on your mind.
Let them take you over,
free your mind and soon you'll see.
The evidence you left behind,
was a trail of crumbs just for me.
Let her open you up,
and pry within, deep inside.
But you will keep it sheltered,
to whom you seem to confide.
Let's melt the cement,
that holds you all together,
the cement that keeps composure,
the stuff that dreams are made of.
Rebuild and reshape it,
as a platform to stand on,
as a plateau to rise up to,

The Stranger Inside

as a new height to reside on.

Rise up the ladder to new worlds,

where freedom's free and people dream.

Cotton candy clouds support your thoughts,

things are always as they seem.

*   *   *

Time passes, and things change drastically for Noah. For the first time since leaving his father's house, Noah has become involved with someone other than himself. Whereas Noah used to spend most of his time alone working on his poetry, now he spends almost all of his time with her.

His apartment has even begun to reflect the changes occurring within and without him. His living room is no longer so bare. A bureau has sprouted next to the desk leading to Noah's room and a small coffee table has appeared before the cheap couch. In the bureau are some new clothes that he bought with her, as well as some of her clothes. Upon the coffee table lies a small collection of gossip magazines of the type which clearly had never before been allowed into Noah's apartment. The kitchen too has miraculously become clean. The sink has been liberated from the oppression of a mountain of dirty dishes, the stovetop has been cleared of grease and the burnt remains of sausage, and the linoleum on the floor shines as though new. Noah's bedroom is no longer quite so spartan. The broken mirror has been replaced by a new unbroken one and another dresser, with more of her things inside, has been put next to the one that was already there. In general, the apartment looked lived in once again. It looked tidy and organized and no longer gave off the distinct and reeking impression of an abode of an artist.

Practically everything Noah did was with her. It was as though they had managed to become one single person in the span of a few short weeks. The few people who knew Noah saw in him a complete transformation. Enrique could barely recognize this new happy and smiling figure constantly asking for an extra place at his usual table in the Café Noir. The landlord of Noah's building had never been given the month's rent with such enthusiasm. Even Mr. Greaves saw a change in Noah.

He was becoming a new man.

* * *

I have no desire to write. I find I am barely able to write even this short little testimonial. She is taking up a greater part of my life now, and I feel no desire, no urge, and no impetus to write. Poetry, my work, was my life for so long. And yet now it seems so irrelevant and unimportant compared to her. I love her. She is my reason and my life; without her I would be absolutely nothing and no one. I would be nothing but a lampshade. In retrospect, I was nothing but a lampshade before she came into my life, I can see that now. My misplaced arrogance and self-loving deluded me and kept me from seeing what a hollow life I was living. But no more. Now she blesses me with her presence.

I have no desire to write. My only desire is to be with her.

* * *

It was raining on the morning of November 30 when Noah awoke to gentle sunlight filtering through his window. It was one such morning where the weather couldn't quite seem to make up its mind as to what it was going to be like. A light rain was falling, but the sun was shining brightly. There was a swift wind stirring up the last of the autumn leaves, but it was not overly cold outside, just wet. She was lying next to him in bed, breathing softly, the sun was starting to peek through his bedroom window, and the room was slowly growing lighter by degrees. Noah took note of all these things as he awoke.

Noah softly got out of bed and went to the kitchen to make himself a cup of tea. He padded his way into the kitchen, his feet armed with slippers against the cold linoleum floor. He began boiling water for tea and stared out of his kitchen window, which overlooked a side street near his building. While gazing out of this window, a creeping feeling started to wash over Noah; it was an anxious feeling coming from the center of his chest, heavy and cold. Noah shuddered and turned away from the window.

Sometime later, she woke up and joined Noah in the kitchen. She didn't speak. Lately, she had taken to falling silent more and more often. This silence was growing more and more concerning to Noah. Whereas the kitchen was once always full of her lively chatter, it was now ominously silent. He noticed this once again, but this time felt unable to simply let the silence pass as he had been doing for some time.

"What's the matter? You barely talk to me anymore."

"Nothing is the matter, Noah."

Silence. It once again pervaded the room. Noah stared hard at the orange pattern on her shirt and started to become irritated.

"Look, don't tell me nothing is the matter when you sit there silently in some kind of piss poor mood refusing to tell me the truth. What's the matter?"

She looked up at Noah and glared. Again, silence. A hard stare and silence.

"God damn it, what is going on!"

"This is the problem, Noah. You don't even know. For practically the past week you haven't known. What is wrong with me? What is wrong with you! You aren't the man you were when I met you."

The Stranger Inside

"What do you mean I'm not the man I was?" Noah cried out becoming more frustrated.

"You aren't the man I met in the café! You aren't the man I was enchanted with in your book! You aren't the man you were in your words, Noah! I didn't notice it at first, but I feel like I'm living with a stranger. You don't even write anymore."

"What the hell is wrong with you? What do you mean I'm not the man I was in my words? Why are you complaining, I don't write as much because I am with you? My work consumed my life before, but now it's you that's more important, so I don't let my work consume me. What have I done wrong?"

"I never asked you to stop writing. I never wanted you to change to accommodate me. I wanted Noah Thompson, the man I saw in the poetry you wrote in your book!"

"I am Noah Thompson!"

"No, you're not. You're some other person, some other man who I don't even have an interest in, some man I don't even know!"

"I changed my whole routine for you! I let you into my apartment, my life! I let you change the way I do things, change a routine I had kept for so long. You opened my eyes to how shallow and arrogant I had been and made me a better man. I changed for you don't you see . . ."

"I never asked you to change!" she cried cutting him off, "I wanted you just the way you were in your book. You aren't Noah Thompson. You're just some flake who I've wasted time with."

Noah roared in anger. "Then why are you here, huh? If I'm such a flake, then get out!"

"Fine, maybe I will!"

"Get out!" Noah screamed.

Grabbing the handle of the teapot that had begun to whistle, Noah hurled it over her head and into the kitchen wall behind her. She screamed and ran out of the kitchen. Noah was in a rage. She had done the unimaginable. She had condemned him for trying to be a better man.

The Stranger Inside

All of Noah's life had been one large and complex lie he had continually told to himself about what was really important, a lie that he continually made himself believe. In finding her, Noah had finally had the veil of illusion lifted from his eyes, only to now be damned by the woman he thought of as his savior for having seen the truth. Noah stormed out of the kitchen and headed to his bedroom. She was hurriedly changing out of her pajamas and throwing random objects of hers haphazardly into her bag. Upon seeing Noah enter the room, she held her bag up like a shield between them.

"Don't you dare come near me, you madman!"

"What's the matter? Scared of me now? Huh? Do I scare you?" Noah said taking short steps toward her with each word.

"Stay away from me! I don't know who you are! You are not Noah Thompson!" She threw her bag at Noah, and while he was momentarily distracted, ran by him and out of the apartment. She would never come back.

*   *   *

This cannot be happening to me. She is gone. This cannot be happening.

She left me. I am at a loss for words. I don't know what to do anymore. Three days ago she left, after a fight we had. I don't even know what the fight was about. Silence? She said I'm not the person she saw in my writing. But what can that mean? Have I not only ever been myself? I was trying to be a better person for her, but it just drove her away. Was she more in love with my writing than with me? God help me I don't know what to do.

I have spent these last few nights pacing my kitchen. I pace, and I drink, and I pace, and now I write this. I don't understand, it was all so wonderful, we were both so happy. Or so I thought. I didn't even want to write anymore because of her; she gave to me a meaning that my work had never been able to. And now she leaves me because I am not the man she saw in my writing. I am not the man in the words. What was in those words that is not in me now? I cannot understand.

She gave my life such meaning. After years of arrogant self-deception I had finally had my eyes opened. She had saved my soul. But now she walks away, and my soul is torn apart. I am rendered nothing more than a ghost. I cannot go back to the man I was, that man is dead. That man was a lie. I cannot be the man I was when I was with her, for she is gone. What am I?

I am the ghost of a shadow of a soul.

I am just an object. Existing. Floating. Being.

I am nothing.

I am a lampshade.

I lost my soul while still living.

God help me, I am becoming my father.

* * *

Life is a stage with no one watching,
they set you up to knock you down.
Build the platforms and your actors.
Learn about their burning automation.
You start your act with emotion.
Acting flawless with strength and conviction.
The act ends as soon as it starts.
And as soon as it ends the new begins.

The Stranger Inside

A flow and an ebb with every beat.

The beat of life follows every noise.

The sound is not heard by any one.

Though the director claims he heard it once.

He speaks of a sound so faint,

so pivotal and full of serenity.

It weaves in and out of every move,

pains and creates new lines for you to follow.

Then the stage clears and you are left

to take your final bow and clean the stage.

The audience gets up to applaud your show.

But no one makes a noise,

no one starts to clap.

They get up and walk away,

as if the pain had taken over.

The sound of silence fills the room,

constricting you and choking you

until everyone has left.

* * *

The month of December was cold. The building in which Noah lived was under siege by the elements. Snow fell frequently and the wind was constantly assailing the leaky and loosely held windows of the building. The three concrete steps leading up to the building's door were iced over and a constant danger to anyone attempting to enter or leave. None of these things were noticed by Noah, for he was taken with his grief at having lost her and at having lost himself.

He had holed himself up in his apartment in precisely the same way that Mr. Greaves did. Now it seems Noah could finally empathize with the pain Mr. Greaves felt. That is, if he chose to take the time to empathize with anyone or anything but himself.

In losing her and once again becoming alone, Noah had completely introverted himself once more. His pain, his loss, his anger, and his frustration consumed his every thought. With each passing day, he grew to hate and love her more. He despised her for having destroyed his new sense of truth in himself, but he loved her with every fiber of his body for having allowed him to lift the veil from his eyes. With each passing day, he became more miserable with himself. Noah was trying to find an inner peace that would allow him to move on and accept that she was gone, but still retain the sense of truth she had given him. He felt unable to do this. He felt trapped and isolated within himself. The one thing Noah desired above all else, and which kept him from sleep, was peace of mind. Peace of mind that would allow him to accept that though his life had previously been a lie, he was as capable of living anew as he had been when with her despite the fact that she was now gone.

Noah was in anguish, and his surroundings began to reflect his anguish, his anxiety. The kitchen managed to almost instantly transform back into the dirty mess it had once been: the sink full of dishes, the stovetop greasy and full of crumbs, and a refrigerator with practically nothing within it. The shards of the teapot he had thrown had not been disturbed since first crashing against the kitchen wall coming to rest upon the floor. There were also a profuse number of empty bottles of gin lying about. These bottles seemed to form a trail leading away from the table in the kitchen to the cheap couch in the living room. The trail never entered Noah's bedroom, for he had not entered it since the moment she ran out of the apartment.

Noah tried to write but with no real success. It seemed that although she was now gone, she had taken with her Noah's ability to write. It seemed to Noah that she had taken away everything from him. She revealed to him the lie that was his life and took away his old routine. She had taken away his desire to write and made him desire only her.

The Stranger Inside

She had taken away the victory of his seeing the truth about himself, and now the better man he had become was a curse. She took away his ability to get back into his work, and now Noah was left without a purpose. She had robbed him of his spirit, and now Noah was lost.

The month of December was cold, but Noah scarcely took notice.

*　*　*

How does a man pick up the threads of a weave when the pattern has been forgotten? One month. One month without her and I am as lost as on the night she first walked out. I have barely slept. I can't fall asleep. I close my eyes, and there she is, taunting me with her presence. I long for her so, and yet seeing her in my mind's eye causes me nothing but pain. For the image I see before my waking eyes is nothing but an illusion, it's nothing but a dream.

I have tried to put my life back together. I sent some garbage to my publisher for review so that I could get an advance on my next book. One year waiting and all I can manage to send to him is garbage not worth reading. Garbage that makes me physically sick when I read it. What else could I do? I am trying to rebuild my life, but I know I am failing. Once the curtain is lifted from a man's eyes, how can he go back into the world of the curtain? I can't go back.

I can't write anymore. Poetry was my work, my life, my soul. Then she came and showed me how I was lying to myself, how the values I had made for myself were made by an illusion, and then she became my soul. Now she is gone, and I am lost. I have lost my soul, it has been misplaced. I have lost the thing most important to me, and I have no idea how I can ever find it again.

The Stranger Inside

My soul has perished, but my body has lingered on. I cannot go on like this.

*   *   *

It is early morning on December 31, and Noah is staring at his kitchen table. In front of him lies a heavy metal strongbox, a chain, a thick padlock, all of his unpublished manuscripts, and his book. His life's work. His life's achievements. His life's lies.

Noah carefully placed all of his manuscripts into the strongbox one page at a time, carefully reading each page as he did so. He grimaced at nearly every page.

Noah then picked up his book. He stared at it for a long time. Stared into its cover as though trying to grasp some meaning hidden from him within the book itself. After a time, he heaved a deep and heavy sigh, and placed the book within the strongbox on top of all the unedited and unpublished papers. Noah then closed and locked the strongbox.

Getting up from the kitchen table he looked around at his apartment. It was cluttered with empty bottles, papers in disarray, and Noah's clothing. Noah picks up the strongbox, the chain, and the padlock and surveys his apartment with steady and sorrowful eyes. The chaos of the apartment did not reflect the calm certitude of Noah's mind. He knew exactly what he had to do. Wrapping the chain around the strongbox he padlocked the awkward amalgamation of metal to his left wrist. With a weary confidence, Noah walked out of his apartment, never to enter it again. Outside, the cab he had called for was waiting. Waiting to take him to the lake just outside the city limits.

We all search for an inner calm in moments of anguish, whether that anguish comes from within us or from without us. Noah had been searching for a way to find that calm and accept the fate he saw before him as inescapable. He had found it, on that early morning of December 31. In that early morning, Noah had found his garden of Gethsemane.

The Stranger Inside

Now he could face his fate with a melancholy tranquility and without fear.

As the cab pulled away from the building Noah would never see again, he didn't look back. Unlike Mr. Greaves, Noah had found a way to let go.

* * *

A broken, shattered soul,
Emancipated from his purpose.
Excavated from the body,
That encompasses his every thought.
A prison he builds,
The warden of his mind.
She left him slowly rotting,
And never looked behind.
A sharp and trolling motion,
To explain his phantom vows.
She'll break him with his cravings
And control him with her strings.
Grief and pity take her reins,
As if they were the same.
Her presence fills his bleeding mind,
But he knows she never came.
A wound of many years before,
Perpetuating anguished dreams.
He feels her hand caress his,
Her poison seeps within.
A clouded mind of scattered thoughts,
Molests him late at night.
She fills him up with emptiness,

The Stranger Inside

While brandishing his sight.
A ribbon flows from her arm,
Created from his flowing thoughts.
She's broken a stoic man,
And leaves him sprawled out on the floor.
He checks for any sign of her,
Within his books and pages.
No trace of her brash existence,
She's left through hell's stages.
Chasing shadows in the night,
His mind is lost in misery.
Left a cold and burning mass,
He's haunted in his sleep.
His thoughts seem singed and distanced,
They are floating with the birds.
And so as these thoughts flow out of him,
They drown him with his words.

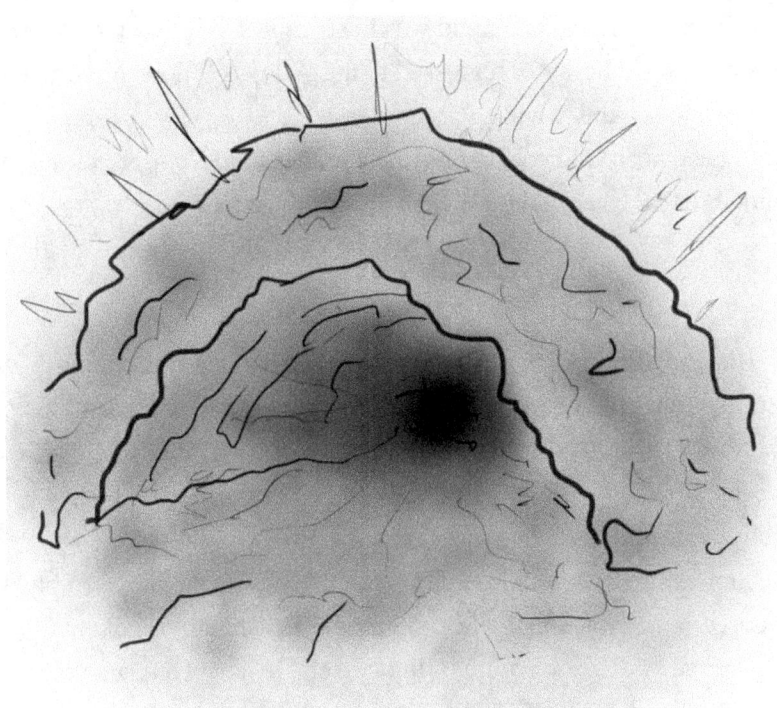

The Gate to Oblivion

He was overcome by anxiety marked by the sense of impending doom. He was falling ceaselessly through space and time. The water was frigid and unforgiving. His mind was in shambles. Air became water, and time stood still. The water regressed to air. All was followed promptly by a sudden impact and fervid agony.

Sebastian, trying to dismiss his trauma, could not recall anything remarkable that could have led to such a predicament.

* * *

His voyages were deliberate and calculated. Each trip was scheduled as a trial of liberation from society. He would spend his time in self-reflection to further his apprehension of the world. Today, however, his thoughts *were* in disarray. His craft was not overly ornate by any account. The wooden structure was built as a capsule of protection not for aesthetic enjoyment. Its minimalistic assembly was composed of several lengths of rigid timber fastened by steel crossbeams to secure the systematic nature of the vessel. He had even handcrafted the boat out of reproach of the pliant designs marketed by conventional retailers.

As he lay across its supports, Sebastian had felt a gust of wind. He knew that a storm was on the horizon, but disregarded its warning. However, the gust grew larger and more rampant. He had feared what was to come, assuming the worst. With this, Sebastian had readied himself for the return voyage. This preparation was met by a gale force wind that overtook him and sent him plummeting toward the abyss that currently harbored him.

The Stranger Inside

Sebastian gathered his strength and found it unsettlingly easy to stand. He began to inspect his confines by the fleeting light that pervaded. It appeared to him that he landed in a cavern of sorts. The walls were formed in intricate patterns from some indiscernible cobbled deposit. The cavern led down a corridor into further darkness. Sebastian felt drawn to the darkness; he felt an overwhelming compulsion that drove his legs farther into the recesses of the cave.

He had not taken more than ten steps before he encountered a site he could never have suspected. In front of him was a door. The door was brilliant and lavish, it exemplified opulence and extravagance. The intricacy of the patterns on the walls paled in comparison to the complexity of what stood before him. The door commanded attention. It stood nearly ten feet tall and was the most vibrant shade of white that man could ever construe. The door was littered with carvings depicting the devil's crusade on heaven and all that it entailed, with a solid line cut diagonally through it, separating the sides.

Offsetting the grandiose nature of the doorway, a man stood attending the door's immaculate hinges. Sensing Sebastian's presence, he twisted his torso in redirection.

"Welcome." The man uttered as the rest of his body pivoted.

"Where am I?"

"That, I cannot answer."

"Why not? I deserve to know where I've been taken," Sebastian said as he slowly approached the man.

"As you know, life is not about what you deserve."

"Well, I demand you tell me what is going on and who you are," Sebastian commanded, further approaching the man.

"I am the gatekeeper, and this is my gate." The gatekeeper said, as he returned to his work.

Sebastian could finally see the man in all his splendor. His suit was as white as snow with a seemingly familiar pattern. His shoes were black and contained the same pattern as the suit. The man's tie was the only article of clothing he wore that differed in pattern. It was a flat black tie with no pattern or design—it was dark and dismal. His hair was slicked back with such precision that it looked as if it was merely painted to his skull.

The austere nature of the man frightened Sebastian, "Where does your door lead?"

"Well, that depends on you now, doesn't it?"

"How could a door's destination depend on me?"

"That, I cannot answer."

Sebastian's temper was mounting. "Stop with the games. Where *can* the door lead?"

The man contorted his torso toward Sebastian, "There are but three destinations to which the door shall deposit you. The first is the place from which you come. The second is a place of eternal perdition. The last is a place of eternal bliss."

Before the gatekeeper could return to his work, Sebastian questioned, "What determines where it will take me?"

"It is not what, but who." The gatekeeper reverted to his natural stature and returned to his task.

"How does that even makes sense? What can I do to affect a door?"

"That, I cannot answer."

Sebastian was losing his temper. He could not stand being treated so disrespectfully. "Can you answer anything constructively at all?" he shouted at the gatekeeper.

"One must first ask the right questions."

"Oh so that's your game. Well if it's questions you want, its questions you'll get."

Sebastian began to question everything he could think of to no avail. Most times, the gatekeeper did not even reply, but occasionally he would let the record play and inform Sebastian that he could not answer the question.

The Stranger Inside

Sebastian grew tired of the game and slowly stopped asking questions. He sat on the ground to think about the questions he had asked and the ones he did not get to. After several minutes of deliberation, he asked the man, "Well then, what should I ask?"

The man replied, "That, I cannot answer."

As the gatekeeper said this, his mouth began to collapse. The separation between his top and bottom lips became blurred, continuing until it was uncertain whether he ever had a mouth at all.

"Well that's just fantastic, what use is there in asking question you won't even answer?" Sebastian said aloud to himself.

The gatekeeper busied himself with his work, as Sebastian rose to his feet.

"Why should I even try if I'll never know if I succeeded?"

Sebastian began to pace. He heard from the distance a response, "Find the answer and you'll be on your way."

"The answer to what? This whole situation is ridiculous. How could a question determine my fate?"

Sebastian began to pound his fists on the wall. "This is unbearable. At least when you could talk I could know that I wasn't on the right track. What's the point anymore . . . what's the point of a life without knowledge?"

Sebastian fell to the ground and began to weep. The tears were slow at first in hopes they would soon subside. The release was too strong for him and began to consume him. Recognizing his outburst and loss of control, he attempted to recollect himself. "I refuse to give up until I figure this out!"

Sebastian threw himself down and lay sprawled out on his back. Staring at the ceiling, he began to think of the life he had lived before this day. He wanted so dearly to return to it. He used to love the mystery of life and the suspense that each day would bring.

Upon this thought he began to become distraught. He sat up and looked at the gatekeeper. He asked the man, "Am I in hell?"

The gatekeeper's body jolted and his head swiveled toward Sebastian. A hole begin to form on the man's face. At first just an opening, then a crevice, and then, as quick as it had disappeared, the gatekeeper's mouth returned.

"That, I cannot answer."

"Great, glad you got your mouth back for that. Now . . ."

The gatekeeper interrupted, "But I must ask, what would prompt such a thought?"

"Well, the way I see it is, this situation is torture, for as long as I allow it. Knowing I won't give up until I succeed at this impossible task ensures that it is eternal."

"But you are permitted to leave at any time," the gatekeeper said, losing confidence.

"That might be true, but where would I go?" Sebastian said, standing up. "Knowing that life is eternal ruins the joy and the value of life. Life is enjoyable, and life is grand because we don't know what is to come afterward. Life is a game, no one remembers who wins or loses at the end, it's not what makes it fun; it's the competition and the experiences encountered within that are the most memorable."

The gatekeeper's body joined his head to listen to what Sebastian had to say.

Sebastian continued, "As for eternal salvation? If happiness and pleasure is all you know, pleasure will become your pain. There is no separation between heaven and hell. Heaven is hell. So really, I'm damned no matter what I choose. And worse yet, even if I don't choose, I'm still damned because I will be eternally stuck with an insurmountable decision. "

The gatekeeper adjusted his tie and straightened his suit.

"What good is anything if you know how it ends? Gatekeeper, I give up. I don't care where that door takes me, because it doesn't matter where it leads. I'm never going to find the answer, and I'm done searching."

The Stranger Inside

"The goal was never to answer the question, just to ask it." The gatekeeper released, handing Sebastian a key.

"Your fate awaits if you're willing to accept it."

Sebastian grabbed hold of the key and put it into the lock. He turned to the gatekeeper as he proceeded through the door.

"I never asked a question. But we both know what it is, because it's the question that drives us. The question is the reason for life. It's man's purpose, and it's the meaning of everything. No one will ever answer the question. No one *can* answer the question. And for that I'm glad, because if it were ever answered, existence would be absurd."

Sebastian proceeded through the ominous door into forever.

* * *

Falling ceaselessly, Sebastian was overwhelmed by anxiety. Falling into the extreme brightness, the palpitations of his heart were the only thing maintaining his consciousness—and as they receded, so did he.

Sebastian awoke in a hallway. Black and white tiles with gold trim outlined a path. White marble walls stood tall, looming over Sebastian and concaved to a point that formed the ceiling.

Sebastian, gathering himself, walked toward the light which drew him and gave him that insatiable urge. He was led down the ornate hallway to a door. A door so red no man could hope to perceive. In front of it stood a man, attending to its hinges.

City on a Hill

The hallway in which the old man was walking resonated with creaks and moans. These noises were so familiar to the old man that they had, in fact, become rather comforting to him. The groans were typical of any structure made of wood that has seen great aging, and both the hallway and the old man had weathered a great many years.

One could only enter the hallway through the east wing door, for the west wing door had been locked some ages ago. Unfortunately, the west wing door could not be unlocked, for the old man had lost the key and has never been able to find it since it first went missing. Upon entering the hallway, one was immediately confronted with its smell. It was a musty old smell with hints of wood polish and the sensation of breathing in old air—as though the hallway had remained closed for a time and was only just opened up again. The hallway could have once been said to smell of freshly cut cedar, but that was a very long time ago. The current odor permeating the place was not unpleasant, but it was pervasive. The hallway was illuminated by ancient gas lamps protruding from the walls. The flickering of the lamps made it seem as though the tiny pockets of shadow strewn amidst the globes of illumination were continuously moving. The old man had once been cheered at the sight of these bits of shadow flitting along the edges of his hallway, but he had now ceased to notice their endless dance. The old man was far too preoccupied now to notice the dancing shadows; he has been for some time.

In many ways the old man's preoccupation has been the cause for the misplacement, and consequent disappearance, of a number of small items: the key to the west wing door being one example. This did not bother the old man, however, for there was little that did bother him. His preoccupation was what concerned him most, and so long as nothing disturbed it he was content. It was, in fact, his preoccupation that brought him to the hallway on such a frequent basis. For you see, the old man was constantly making models.

*   *   *

"Well," sighed the old man to himself as he opened the east wing door and walked into the hallway, "Here we are once again."

The musty smell of the hall pervaded his nostrils as he slowly walked down the long hallway, the floorboards creaking under his weight as he walked. Passing by door after door on both sides, the old man didn't take his eyes off his shuffling feet. Upon reaching the middle of the hallway, he turned to look at the bureau of drawers on his right, sighed, and looked away. The old man eventually reached his destination, one of the many doors lining the entire hallway.

He stopped and looked at the door for a moment—a hopeful gleam in his eyes. Reaching into his vest pocket, he pulled out a small and slightly rusted key and stared at it with the same hopeful look.

"This time, this time I shall get it right," thought the old man as he reached out, unlocking the door, "this time it shall be perfect."

As the hall door opened, the old man surveyed the room beyond the door. Everything seemed to be just as he left it. Directly in front of him and across the room was the large oak table holding the model city; to its right and left were the bins containing the multitude of items he used to make, expand, and change the model. On the right wall was a fireplace and beside the fireplace was his weathered green leather armchair. On the left wall was the large bookcase with shelves filled with the unpainted figurines he was slowly placing into his current model. Satisfied that nothing had been changed, the old man turned and locked the door behind him and, placing the key back into his vest pocket, walked over to the large model city that dominated the room.

The Stranger Inside

The model city itself was very large. It spanned nearly seven feet in length and another four feet in width. Next to the model, strewn about the sides of the table, were many of the old man's tools and little shavings of wood and other bits and bobs left over from the previous day's alterations. He circled the table once just to make sure his tools were as he had left them and then began to take a closer look at the model city itself.

The old man suddenly began to frown.

"It can't be, has it changed again?" The old man thought as he squinted and moved in closer to one section of the city so as to get a better look.

Upon closer inspection, it became immediately apparent to him that, once again, the model city had changed without the guidance of the old man.

The old man's frown deepened.

"I will not allow this."

The old man bent over a particular section of the model city and began making rapid and quick alterations to the model's structure. He hoped, as he always did, that with quick and surgical manipulations, he would be able to restore the model city to the near-perfect state in which he had left it. He was most annoyed and disheartened. When first entering the room, he had been hopeful that perhaps today the model would not have undergone unguided alterations, but once again the figurines had proved themselves too unwilling to follow instruction.

* * *

The creation of each of the old man's models always followed a similar pattern. It always began with raw imagination—that was the key. It was, in fact, the old man's imagination that had been fueling his preoccupation for so many long years. First, he would sit in the green leather armchair and imagine the basic structure of the city itself. Then,

122

he would imagine the pattern the city blocks would take throughout the allotted space the model was to occupy, and slowly, he would begin to fill those spaces. One block at a time, the environment of the model would start to take shape. This process of building the city structure itself usually took the old man no more than two days. After so many long years of practice, he had become a master of creating city structures.

The layout and design of the various city models was always an object of pride to him. They were designed so artfully and with such grace and subtlety that it would seem that the city grew on its own—like a seed germinating into the most beautiful and complex of trees. The many intersecting city lanes seemed natural outgrowths of the major roads and squares of the city. The buildings seemed to span a variety of seemingly incompatible architectural styles and yet melded perfectly with one another. Dotted throughout the city were the small number of compact and yet quite spaciously tranquil parks full of copious greenery which brought a more natural feel to the concrete-and-stone city.

In essence, the city structures of the old man's models were always perfect. Like single snowflakes, each was uniquely elegant and irreplaceable. The problem which the old man continually faced when creating his models, therefore, had nothing to do with the structure of the city itself, but rather dealt with the figurines.

For you see, the old man was not simply content with creating perfect model cities, for this had become too easy. He was now determined to populate these perfect cities with perfect people. But this was proving more difficult than he had ever imagined.

The problem facing the old man was simple: the figurines were rejecting much of his guidance.

*   *   *

The Stranger Inside

Bent over the one section of the city, the old man concentrated his effort on making repairs to the buildings and other structures that the painted figurines must have damaged in his absence.

"Always the same. Why don't you all listen to me?" said the old man aloud, addressing the figurines, "I create the perfect city for you all in not but two days and off you go damaging it."

No reply.

"Of course, I may as well be talking to air. You all stop listening once you're painted."

The old man stopped his work and straightened up for a moment to stretch. While stretching, his eye caught sight of the bookshelf of unpainted figurines in his peripheral vision. He sighed to himself rather deeply and walked slowly over to the fireplace and stared for a moment into the embers of the fire.

"Six days since I lit the fire. Only one day left before it is extinguished, and they are out of my hands."

The old man turned to look again at the model then at the bookshelf.

"They are so much more obedient when left unpainted," he thought to himself, "and yet so much more lifeless too."

Glancing once more at the slowly dying fire, "I still have one day left. I can still save them."

He rushed back over to the model and began to repair the damaged sections with a zealously renewed effort.

* * *

The old man had always had a plan in mind for his models; he always had a design carefully mapped out and crafted to make each model city a paragon of perfection. The problem was that certain key elements of his perfect design never quite worked out as he had imagined once the figurines were painted and placed into the model city.

124

The Stranger Inside

Certain sections of the city were always damaged during the old man's absence. Thankfully, the damage done was always limited to a few places and was not so rampantly widespread throughout the entire model. If the damage had ever been so great, there would have been no hope of the old man ever creating the perfect model city. But while the damage was limited it still detracted from the model's perfection, and thus, the old man did his best to repair the model faster than the figurines could damage it. He had yet to be successful in this endeavor.

There was also the issue of the figurines, many of whom refused to fulfill their assigned purpose. Each figurine was perfectly designed to fulfill a purpose within the model and through the fulfillment of that purpose, attain happiness. The old man had painted the figurines specifically so they could see themselves as unique and better sense their happiness; such was the original purpose of the paint. Now, however, the figurines had taken their new power of awareness and decided to ignore his guidance whenever they so chose. They went off and damaged the city; they choose alternate, and sometimes self-destructive, paths for themselves; and they often ignored the purpose the old man had assigned to them entirely.

The old man was powerless to stop this, for once a figurine was painted and placed within the model, it could not be altered. All that the old man could do to try to mitigate the manner in which the figurines chose to behave was to alter the environment of the model itself or, in those extreme cases when a particular figurine was proving to be too troublesome, remove a figurine from the model. He hated having to remove any of his figurines though, for in doing so, the removed figurine would never be able to reenter the model and would have to remain next to its unpainted brethren on the bookshelf. This was an assured way of making the painted figurine miserable, for it would be fully aware of its entrapment among the calm and unthinking mass of unpainted figurines. For the old man, creating perfect people for his perfect model meant that the people would always be happy, and he hated having to make any of his figurines suffer. It was for this reason that he tried so hard to fix the constantly changing model.

*   *   *

The old man pulled out his handkerchief and mopped the sweat off his brow. As he straightened himself up, his back cracking, he surveyed the model city. He allowed himself a small smile, for the long day's work seemed to have paid off.

"Damage repaired, particularly important figurine's environments realigned and set on the right path, all has been put right," he thought to himself. "Now they await the arrival of the last figurine."

Looking toward the bookshelf, the old man stared at the unpainted figurine he had set aside when he first began the model. He was sure that this was the only figurine with the right set of qualities to be the perfect leader of his perfect city. He was still somewhat uneasy, however, for the last figurine was arguably the most important. For it was the last figurine who possessed the power to lead the model city to the path of perfection or, if corrupted, down the path of ruin. It was for this reason that the old man always painted this figurine last, for he knew only too well how easily the last figurine can be corrupted if placed into a model too soon.

The old man walked over to the bookshelf and tenderly took the last figurine in his hand and walked back over to the model.

"Tomorrow, all this will be yours."

After a moment, the old man turned away from the model and carefully placed the last figurine back on the shelf. He then walked over to the fireplace and peered once more into the embers.

"By this time tomorrow, it will be spent. By this time tomorrow," he turned to glance at the model city, "it will possess a life of its own."

Taking out his handkerchief to mop up the last few stray beads of sweat from his face, the old man walked over to the door. Reaching into his vest pocket, he pulled out the small and slightly rusted key and unlocked the door. His hand on the doorknob, he turned to look back at the model city and at the last figurine.

"Tomorrow, all that will be yours. I can only hope that you are ready to enter it and that it is ready to receive you."

With a quick motion of his hand, the old man opened the door, left the room, and shut the door behind him. He then reinserted the key and locked the door. Placing the key back into his vest pocket, the old man walked down the hallway and away.

From within the room, the slight click of the door being locked was also heard by the figurines.

*   *   *

It was always during the absence of the old man that the figurines truly came to life. While they chose to no longer hear the old man, they were generally aware of his presence. They were also generally aware of the fact that they were within the model, within his creation. They were far less aware, however, of the fact that they too were his creations.

This was always their way, so it had been since the very first model. During the seven days that the fire burned, they were still linked to the old man, linked to the world beyond the model city. This link allowed them to perceive, at once, both their environment within the model as well as the world beyond. Thus, the figurines knew they were within a place created by a presence from the world outside. But once painted, it never occurred to them that they too were made in the world outside and then placed into this world that they had come to be aware of.

And so one can see how the figurines might be inclined to rebel against the guidance they were receiving from this outside presence, this presence that seemed to have captured them and placed them on display. The painting of the figurines gave them awareness and made them feel unique and alive, but it also made them far more self-absorbed. The figurines, once painted, seemed to lose sight of the larger picture. They could not see the end result of the guidance given to them by the old man, too saturated as they were in the environment of the model. They could not see the possibility of perfection as he saw it.

But then, how could they? After all, they were just figurines.

* * *

With the click of the key turning in the lock, the old man opened the door to the room. He took a moment to survey the room. Everything seemed to be just as he left it. Satisfied that nothing had been changed, the old man turned and locked the door behind him and, placing the key back into his vest pocket, walked over to the bookshelf and tenderly picked up the last figurine.

"It is time."

Placing the last figurine on the edge of the table next to the model, the old man made a more detailed inspection of the sections of the city he had repaired on the previous day.

The old man suddenly began to frown.

"Well, clearly not quite time yet."

The old man picked up the last figurine and placed it back on the bookshelf. Turning back to the model, he sighed. Not only had the sections he had just repaired the day before returned to a state of disarray, but a number of new sections of the city had also been damaged. The old man was greatly frustrated. He knew that time was now against him. He knew he could not repair the sections of the city he had fixed before, repair the newly damaged sections, and paint the last figurine in the time left to him by the rapidly dying fire—at least not to the degree of perfection which he wished. The old man sighed again.

"For what reason have you all done this? Now my great work has been slowly undone, and you force me to leave imperfections among you."

No reply.

"I have so little time now." He took a quick look at the fireplace. "So little time."

Picking up a few tools, the old man immediately set to work at a frenetic pace. He had to make careful decisions about which sections of the model city were the most crucial and would need to be repaired and which sections he would be forced to abandon. He was greatly displeased at having to abandon any section of the city, but the figurines had given him no choice, or rather, presented to him a choice he did not want to make.

In such a circumstance, the old man had only three options. He liked none of them, but as of late, he had resigned himself to the lesser of three evils. He could accept that certain damaged parts of the city would have to be abandoned and left imperfect so as to be able to place the last figurine in the model in time; he could choose to not place the last figurine in the model at all and save as much of the city as he could before time ran out; or he could refuse to accept the model in any state but that of perfect and destroy it completely. As he worked on what he had decided were the key sections of the model, the old man thought about the choices he had made in the past.

In his more ardent and zealous days, the old man had taken the third option when presented with a situation such as this one. He remembered those days with something akin to shame and guilt. It was not too long before the old man could no longer bear to utterly end his creations in such a way. It was then that he attempted the second option and left the model without a leader, without the last figurine. He only ever attempted this option once. The model city fell to corruption and disarray so quickly and with such awful consequences that the old man was horrified at what he had done. He vowed to never leave the city without the last figurine ever again. This vow, and his inability to destroy his creations in the ways of the past, left him with the first of the three options.

"Better this way," he thought to himself. "Better they live among a few imperfections than are destroyed or left to such desolate ruin."

Realizing he had allowed himself to become distracted from his work, the old man focused himself and returned to the repairs.

"Well, I suppose that will have to do."

The old man made a cursory survey of the repairs he had made and then looked at the fire. He did not even take a moment to mop the sweat from his brow, but went directly over to the last figurine.

"Now, it is time."

With the last figurine in one hand and his set of paints and brushes in the other, the old man walked over to the green leather armchair and sat down. Now, for the first time since he had entered the room that day, he paused for a moment and thought deeply.

The painting of any figurine was always a delicate business that could not be rushed, and this was especially the case for the last figurine. Absolutely no mistakes could be made in the brushstrokes without completely compromising the integrity of the figure. The old man turned the last figurine over in his hands and allowed an image of what it should look like once painted to form in his mind.

"Yes, that's it," he said aloud, smiling, "I have an image for you."

Slowly, and with great care, the old man began to paint the last figurine.

He began with the physical elements of the body. With deft strokes, he gave the last figurine flesh, then a nose and a mouth and ears and hair. Stopping for a moment to switch brushes and to allow it to dry, the old man looked at the figurine.

"Yes, coming along very nicely. A rather regal countenance of the face."

The old man then began to give the last figurine clothes. Socks, shoes, underclothes, dark black pants, a shirt with a tie, cufflinks, and a suit jacket suddenly began to emerge. The old man smiled, for he was quite pleased with the figurine's appearance.

"You cut quite the figure, don't you?" he chuckled a little to himself.

The old man put down the brushes he had been using and gave the figurine a moment to dry—he took that moment to compose himself. The most important part of the painting still lay ahead, the giving of the eyes. It was the eyes that made the figurine aware, that allowed it to become much more than the calm and unthinking mass of its unpainted brethren. It was the eyes that made the figurine. Composed and ready, the old man began the giving of the eyes.

"There! You are ready."

The old man jumped out of the green leather armchair and moved swiftly over to the edge of the model. He had but a few precious moments to insert the last figurine into the model while it was still disoriented from the giving of the eyes. With one quick yet careful movement, the last figurine was placed in the center of the model on the grand platform of the city square. It was there, in the middle of the city, that the last figurine became aware of itself. It was then, at the moment that the last figurine opened its eyes, that the fire went out.

The old man took a step back to look at the model in its entirety. He did not need to look at the fire to know that it had been extinguished, for he felt the link between himself and his creations severed the moment the fire died.

"Now, in these first few moments it will be decided if I have at long last succeeded in my endeavor. Now, we shall see if they choose to reestablish the link between us."

The figurines slowly began to move about. No longer were they at all aware of the old man or of his world now that the fire had died. No longer were they able to feel his presence—that was now just a memory. It was the old man's perpetual hope that the memory of the link between creator and creation would prompt them to reestablish it for themselves, thus at last making them the perfect people for his perfect city. Alas, it had yet to happen.

The old man fidgeted with his hands, staring down at the figurines moving about in his model city. He could see that all memory of the link which once resided in the minds of his figurines was fast fading.

"Come now. Do not fail me. Give me just one success, and I will be content."

The old man looked hopefully upon the last figurine, the leader. He desperately hoped that this figurine would be able to lead the others in reestablishing the link.

"Come now. I cannot do it for you, or you would be no better than your unpainted brethren," the old man said aloud. And then, in a soft whisper, "Please."

No reply.

*　*　*

The old man walked up to the door of the room and unlocked it. He then turned and looked upon the model city for the last time. With a quick motion of his hand, he opened the door, left the room, and shut the door behind him. He then reinserted the key and locked the door forever. Placing the key back into his vest pocket, the old man walked down the hallway.

The musty smell of the hall pervaded his nostrils as he slowly walked down the long hallway, the floorboards creaking under his weight as he walked. Passing by door after door on both sides, the old man didn't take his eyes off his shuffling feet. Upon reaching the middle of the hallway, he turned to look at the bureau of drawers on his left. Stopping, he opened up the third drawer down on the bureau's right side. The drawer was filled with small and slightly rusted keys. Sighing, the old man reached into his vest pocket and took out the key to the door of the room which housed his most recent failure. Looking at the key, there was no hopeful gleam in his eye. The old man placed this key alongside the many others within the drawer.

Closing that drawer, he opened one directly to its left. This drawer was filled with placards. Reaching in, the old man picked up a specific one, looked at it for a moment, closed the drawer, and walked back toward the door whose key he had just placed into the bureau. Upon reaching the door he looked up slightly at the placard already hanging there: CITY OF EARTH – MODEL NUMBER 422 (IN CONSTRUCTION). The old man reached up and took the placard down and replaced it with the one he had fetched from the bureau: CITY OF EARTH – MODEL NUMBER 422 (ABANDONED).

The old man then walked down the hallway once again and stopped at the bureau of drawers. Opening the fourth drawer down on the bureau's right side, he deposited the placard he had taken from the door. He then went to the bureau's left side and opened the second drawer down. This drawer held blank placards. Taking one from the drawer, the old man reached into his shirt's breast pocket and took out his fountain pen. He placed the placard on the top of the bureau and wrote a few words. Placing the fountain pen back in his pocket, the old man looked at what he had written. Satisfied, he closed the drawer which held the blank placards and opened the drawer directly beneath it. The drawer too was filled with small and slightly rusted keys. Picking up a specific one, the old man placed it in his vest pocket, closed the drawer, and picked up the placard.

The old man then turned around and walked back toward the door which held the abandoned model. Upon reaching the door, the old man sighed and then kept walking. The old man soon reached his destination, for it was the door just after the one where he had locked away his latest model.

He stopped and looked at the door for a moment, a hopeful gleam in his eyes. He then took the newly made placard and placed it on the top of the door. The placard read: CITY OF EARTH – MODEL NUMBER 423 (IN CONSTRUCTION). Reaching into his vest pocket, he pulled out the small and slightly rusted key he had just taken from the bureau and stared at it with the same optimistic look with which he had stared at the door.

"This time, this time I shall get it right," thought the old man as he reached out, unlocking the door. "This time, it shall be perfect."

A special thanks to all of those who made this book possible. Just having it published is a dream come true.